I0777977

inflatable furniture and holy water."

-Stephanie Sanders-Jacob, author of *Pyramidia*

"*Birthday Party Demon* delivers! Whether this is your first foray into teen horror, or a nostalgic trip down Fear Street, this book has the chills, creep outs, and chaos you're looking for. Old school thrill seekers will enjoy buddy-reading this book with the next generation of horror fans."

-Joanna Monahan, award-winning author of
Something Better

"Dalrymple delivers a pink horror exorcism you'll be totally bummed to finish!"

-Damien Casey, author of *Church of Skatan*

"A nonstop nostalgic '90s nightmare, *Birthday Party Demon* is a Lisa Frank-tinted thrill ride from beginning to end. I couldn't put it down."

-Robbie Dorman, author of *This Book is Cursed*

"*Birthday Party Demon* is a 90s-drenched fashionista nightmare well worth losing yourself in. It's a perfect ode to the very real anxieties of teenagerdom, tightly-paced and scary fun with a demonic candy coating."

-T.T. Madden, author of

The Familialists and *The Cosmic Color*

"*Birthday Party Demon* reads like if your favorite dea-dite found a creepy, glittery scrunchie, then RSVPed yes to your super sweet sixteen. Dalrymple throws a fun, loud, sparkly party with the best of them."

-William Sterling, author of

Our Beanie Beastie Nightmare

Published by Mad Axe Media

madaxemedia.com

The Totally Freaked! series is an original creation of Mad Axe Media.

Edited by Joey Powell

Book Cover & Interior Design by Joey Powell

Print ISBN: 978-1-966497-04-2

Ebook ISBN: 978-1-966497-05-9

CHRISTMAS PARTY DEMON

Chapter One

Tina, Lacey and Eve were friends. *Best* friends. That is, until Lacey became possessed by a demon at Tina's Sweet Sixteen sleepover birthday party. Ever since that fateful night when they cracked open a Ouija board and recited a cursed spell, things just weren't the same for the three friends. *Lacey* wasn't the same. The demon Zozo—now called Zoey—made itself at home in Lacey's skin, and for Tina and Eve, high school had become a living hell.

It was the last week before Christmas, and the school day had just begun for Tina and her best friend Eve. A chilling December wind whipped down the breezeway of Tropic Acres High School as the two friends trudged toward their lockers. It had been an unusually cold winter in the Sunshine State, and the high school students poured into the open hallways, shivering beneath too-thin jackets and shorts. Tina and Eve spun the dials to their combination locks as a group of boys in flannels, hoodies, and oversized denim jeans crushed in next to them. Eve shoved the boys away as Tina hugged her backpack to her chest and leaned against the lockers.

"Ugh, rude!" Eve said. "Learn about personal space, jerk wads!"

"Ignore them," Tina said. "How did you do on your Geometry final?"

"Mr. Pike gave me a C minus, can you believe that? A C minus!" Eve groaned, shoving books into her bag. "My dad is gonna be so pissed."

"I wish my parents would be pissed about something. Or happy. Or noticed anything about me at all," Tina said. "Miss Martin gave me a D in Gym because I didn't want to dress out. I showed my mom my report card. She didn't even blink."

Tina opened her locker and pulled out a thick World History book. Behind her, a wall of students chattered, nearly drowning out the piped-in Christmas music overhead.

"Dressing out for gym class is dumb," Eve agreed. "Although it's kind of annoying to play volleyball in my fishnets."

"True. Ugh, I'm so ready for winter break," Tina said. "Two weeks away from this place won't be long enough."

Eve nodded. "Me too. Are you going to your Dad's again this year?"

"Yeah, he's not picking me up until Monday, though," Tina said. "My Mom will probably make me meet her new boyfriend before I leave. Gross."

"That Rick guy?" Eve wrinkled her nose. "Isn't he the manager at TGI Fridays?"

"Regional Manager." Tina stuck out her tongue and made a gagging sound. "My Mom is totally obsessed with him. I'll probably be stuck watching them make out all weekend."

"Wanna hang at my place instead?" Eve asked. "We could have a sleepover, make Christmas cookies. It'll be fun."

Tina cringed. An icy finger tapped her spine as memories of her ill fated birthday party sleepover flashed before her eyes. "You think a sleepover is a good idea?"

"Come on, T. It won't be like last time."

"Okay, but no board games." Tina laughed, but she was only half-joking.

Eve held up a hand. "Deal."

Tina slapped her a high-five. An old fashioned rendition of *Hark! The Herald Angels Sing* wafted through halls, echoing over the crowd of rowdy teenagers. Tina closed her locker door and covered her ears. "Don't you think it's weird that they play Christmas music in the halls between classes?"

"What's wrong with Christmas music?" Eve asked. "I mean, I'd rather they turn the radio station to 97X, but I'll take what I can get."

"Like, all this music about God and Baby Jesus," Tina said. "It's just weird. Not everyone at school believes in that stuff."

"Well, I do," Eve said. "Christmas is my favorite."

"Really?" Tina wrinkled her nose. "I thought you were too cool for Christmas."

"No way," Eve said. "Maybe I'm not so sure about all the God stuff, but I definitely celebrate Gothmas."

"Har har."

"Seriously though, all that churchy music is just

words and sounds. It doesn't mean anything," Eve said.

"Words have meaning," Tina said. "Anyway, I just think school should be more inclusive. They're supposed to keep religious stuff out."

"If my family had it their way, religion would be part of every school curriculum." Eve rolled her eyes toward the overhead speakers. "My uncle would love this, especially since he thinks I'm going to go to hell for listening to secular music and for dressing this way."

"How does he know what kind of music you listen to?"

"He was over at the house yesterday and found my Ministry cassette." Eve cringed. "He got excited for a minute and thought I was listening to church sermons on tape."

"Oops."

"He threw the cassette away when he realized what it was. My parents were so embarrassed. They're forcing me to go to church every Wednesday and Sunday now." Eve tugged at her faded black Soundgarden t-shirt. "And I can't wear anything like this around the family anymore."

"Sorry," Tina said. "I know how it feels to have to hide yourself."

Eve pulled her into a side hug. "I know."

BRRRRING!!!

Tina jumped at the sound of the late bell. Students scattered into classrooms and the hallway emptied as another blast of arctic air pushed through the open hallway.

"Crap, gotta run." Eve slung her backpack over her shoulder. "Save me a seat at lunch?"

"You know it."

In past years, Tina dreaded home room, but now, it was one of the only classes that felt safe. Lacey—or rather, Zoey—and her horde of followers infiltrated almost every other period of her school day. Tina bolted for the classroom door and slipped into her seat as her homeroom teacher started the roll call.

"Nolan, Richard," Mrs. Mehdi said.

"Here." Richie Nolan yawned and raised a lazy hand.

"Nyleberg, Elise," Mrs. Mehdi said.

"Here!" Elise Nyleberg raised her hand high and pumped it back-and-forth.

Tina snorted. Elise was always such a suck up.

"MacDonnell, Melissa," Mrs. Mehdi said.

"hErE!"

The blood drained from Tina's legs and her feet went numb. She swiveled and slowly turned her head toward the high-pitched, sing-songy voice coming from Missy MacDonnell's assigned seat. Mousy Missy, as their cruel classmates used to call her in middle school. Tina had never considered Missy to be mousy, just quiet and shy. Reserved. Missy typically wore her shoulder-length brown hair in a ponytail and dressed in a uniform of t-shirts and jeans. Today, however, Missy was sporting a new pixie style haircut and wore a bright, fuzzy rainbow stripe sweater with matching pink pleather pants—the same bright, obnoxious ensemble that Tina had definitely seen in the dARiA*s winter catalog.

"Martin, Christina."

Tina's blood pumped fast and hard in her neck as she stared at the back of Missy's head.

Oh no. Not Missy, too.

"Martin, Christina."

Tina couldn't hear her teacher call after her, but only stared open-mouthed at her classmates' alarming new makeover. She struggled to keep her composure as a million questions ran through her mind.

How many students has Zoey turned into catalog model demons now? Twenty? Thirty? When will it end?

"Christina!"

Tina jumped as Mrs. Mehdi called her name for the third time. The entire classroom turned around to glare. Heat crept up Tina's neck as she gingerly raised her hand.

"Here."

"Thank you for paying attention, Christina." Mrs. Mehdi rolled her eyes. "Mitchel, David."

Tina sank low in her seat, trying to make herself invisible. Mrs. Mehdi finished the roll call, and for the rest of the class, Tina could only stare at Missy's fuzzy rainbow stripe sweater. To anyone else in the classroom, Missy's new look wouldn't seem out of the ordinary, but Tina knew that her style upgrade was likely a sign of something sinister.

It felt like only yesterday when she and Eve discovered that their best friend was still a demon who looked, acted and dressed like a model straight from a fashion catalog. Worse, it seemed like Lacey, now the demonic Zoey, had spread her Ouija board demon virus to some of the students at school. At first, Zoey only seemed to target the popular kids at school, giving them all trendy new demonic makeovers from the inside out. But then she moved on to the softball team, and now it seemed like she had gotten her hooks in Missy MacDonnell as well.

The bell rang again and Tina wandered through the rest of her school day like a zombie. She had already taken most of her finals for the semester, so her classes were fairly easy. Her Physics teacher showed a movie on the roll cart and in Gym class everyone just sat on the bleachers while Miss Martin gave a pop quiz on cardiovascular health. Finally, lunch rolled around, and Tina and Eve were reunited.

"What's on the menu today?" Eve slid next to Tina and plopped her tray on the cafeteria table. Tina eyed Eve's rectangular-shaped pizza, fruit salad, and chocolate milk with envy.

"Ham and cheese on rye. No mayo because we ran out," Tina said. "Wanna trade?"

"No way. Pizza day is the only time this cafeteria food is edible," Eve said. "So I take it you saw Missy, huh?"

"Yep," Tina said. "How many kids does that make now?"

"Probably almost fifty."

Eve and Tina turned their attention to the front of the cafeteria. Zoey held court at her usual spot, surrounded by a gaggle of fashionable, brain-dead students. She flipped her shining flaxen hair over her shoulder and smiled, her teeth bigger and whiter than ever. That day, she was wearing crisp white jeans and a pink sweater. She wore pink all the time now. Lacey used to hate the color pink. Tina's heart ached every time she caught sight of her old friend. The shell of her old friend, anyway. She knew Lacey was still in there somewhere, but with every passing day, hope of getting her back seemed to slip further and further away.

"We have to do something," Tina said. "Before we know it, Zoey is going to turn the entire school into a horde of mindless, demonic fashionistas."

"What can we possibly do?" Eve said. "We tried to perform an exorcism, remember?"

"You all talking about the dead heads over there?" Deon planted his lunch tray on the table and slid into the seat next to Eve. She tugged at the collar of his black trench coat and motioned for him to plant a kiss on her cheek. "Hey babe."

"Yeah," Eve said. "They got Mousy Missy too."

"Don't call her that," Tina said. "Nice jacket, D. It makes you look like a vampire. Where'd you get it?"

"That new store in the mall," Deon said. "They have a bunch of cool band tees and patches and bumper stickers and stuff."

"Anyway, yeah," Eve said. "Tina thinks we need to try another exorcism before Zoey recruits the rest of the student body."

"I don't think I can get Ras to help us again this time," Deon said. "That botched exorcism scared him half to death."

"He didn't know what he was doing anyway." Eve rolled her eyes. "Really, though, what can we do?"

Tina glanced across the cafeteria at Zoey. The demon stared back at her through Lacey's eyes. She smiled a wide, wicked grin that made Tina's blood freeze in her veins.

"We have to try something," Tina said. "Before it's too late."

Chapter Two

The dismissal bell rang, and students sped through the hallways of Tropical Acres High School toward their buses, cars, and bikes. A man with a lounge singer's voice crooned about the most wonderful time of the year, the spirited holiday song echoing through the hallways over the crackling school intercom speakers. Deon and Eve held hands as Tina followed them to the student parking lot where Eve's purple Dodge Neon was waiting. Students chattered amongst themselves about the new sneakers and CD's they wanted to get for Hanukkah and Christmas, where they were going for the holidays, and how happy they were going to be to sleep in for two whole weeks. Everyone was in a cheerful mood; everyone except for Tina.

"The most wonderful time of the year. Yeah right," Tina said. "Seriously, what's so good about it? Can't anyone see what's going on around here?"

Eve opened the driver's side door of her car and popped the locks for Deon and Tina. "I mean, I get why you're being a Scrooge, but T, there's really nothing we can do about it."

"Zoey is going to turn everyone into dead heads," Tina said. "Our entire graduating class is going to be demonic if we don't do *something*."

"Face it, Tina. Most people don't care." Deon slid into the passenger seat. "They'll happily let their souls get sucked out so long as they're cool and popular."

As if on cue, Zoey and her main crew of demonic followers sashayed into the parking lot. Eve, Tina, and Deon sunk low in their seats as the parade of fashionable teens strutted by. Zoey was linked arm-in-arm with Chris Parker, the pitcher from the boys baseball team. Chris was sporting spiky new highlights and a navy snowboard-style sweater with a giant yellow stripe across the chest. His normally dark brown eyes glowed.

"Welp, looks like she got to Chris too," Eve said.

Tina's heart sank. "Are they dating?"

"Wasn't he dating Ashley Spencer?" Deon asked.

"Yeah," Tina said. "Ashley has been one of Zoey's followers for a while now."

"Brutal," Deon said.

"Chris has a nice car," Eve said. "Guess Zoey was sick of taking the bus."

Tina craned her neck to see Chris open the passenger door of his red Hyundai Tiburon. She sighed as her demon-possessed friend and secret crush slipped into the passenger seat of the coolest car driven by the coolest guy at school. Even after all this time, it still hurt her to know that Lacey was likely lost forever behind Zoey's evil glowing eyes. Even if her crush would never be requited, Tina still missed her friend and wasn't ready to give up on her. She pushed her broken heart aside to make room for the anger that bubbled up in her chest.

"There's gotta be something we can do," Tina said. "Deon, are you sure that Ras won't help us?"

"Definitely," Deon said. "Whenever we hang out, he straight up refuses to talk to me about that night."

"Well, there has to be someone who can help us," Tina said. "Eve, do you know anyone?"

Eve started the car and heavy metal music blasted from the speakers. Tina jumped and covered her ears.

"Sorry!" Eve turned the music down. "What about Ras's mom?"

"The lady at the candle shop?" Tina's eyebrows raised. "The one at the mall?"

"I dunno," Deon said. "She's, like, a hippie type of lady. She only messes with incense and simmering pots of herbs and stuff. I don't think she's into the dark arts."

"But she *is* a witch, right?" Eve asked. "Ras may have flunked out of Witchcraft 101, but his mom probably knows a thing or two."

"It's worth a try," Tina said. "I have to work tonight, but maybe we can go to the mall tomorrow after school."

"I need to finish some Christmas shopping anyway," Eve said. "Let's do it."

Tina leaned back in her seat and watched the world go by as Eve drove out of the school parking lot toward her home. Her neighborhood wasn't far from the high school, but Eve was happy to give her a lift all the same. As Eve pulled into Tina's driveway, all three friends gasped. When they left for school that morning, Tina's house was the only one on the block that hadn't been decorated for Christmas. Now, the facade of Tina's little suburban three bedroom, two bath home looked like a regular winter wonderland.

"Did your mom… decorate?" Eve asked.

"I don't recognize any of this stuff." Tina sighed.

"Are you mad about it?" Deon asked. "It looks pretty rad to me."

"No, I'm not mad," Tina said. "I have no idea where all this stuff came from, though."

"What time do you get off work tonight?" Eve asked.

"Nine," Tina said. "Can you still pick me up?"

"Yeah, I'll be there," Eve said. "Later."

"Later."

Tina got out of the car, dazed at the transformation of her home. Ever since her parents' divorce, Tina's mom had given up on a lot of things she used to do, like decorating for the holidays. Something was going on. Her spine tingled and hair stood on end at the possibility of what she might be coming home to.

A wave of vanilla and cinnamon scented air hit her nose as Tina opened the front door. One of her mother's old Christmas records softly spun on the turntable and their artificial Fraser fir tree was propped up in the corner of the living room. Her mother rounded the corner wearing a green and red apron, her hair and makeup all done up like she was getting ready to sit for a portrait at Olan Mills.

"Tina! You're home!" Her mother cupped her face in her hands and planted a kiss on her cheeks. "I just took a batch of Snickerdoodles out of the oven."

"Mom... what's going on?" Tina frowned and gave her mother a skeptical glare. "Why are you home?"

"It's Christmastime! I wanted to take a few days off from work to enjoy the holiday season."

"Okay...Well, where did all of those decorations come from?" Tina slipped her backpack onto the floor. Something was off. Something bad.

"Isn't it great? Rick came over today and surprised me! He knew how much I missed having decorations on the house for the holidays."

"How nice." Tina suppressed the urge to roll her eyes.

"I thought we could have some cookies and decorate the tree when you got home." Her mother picked up a box with the words TINA ORNAMENTS scrawled on the side. "See? I got your old ornaments out and everything."

Tina's mom pulled out a small package from inside the box and opened the lid. Inside was a shining silver ornament in the shape of an angel with the word

"Christina" engraved on it in cursive script. Like Tina, the ornament was also sixteen years old.

"My baby ornaments? We don't have to put those up," Tina said. "Anyway, I can't decorate now. I have to go get ready for work."

"Oh, pooh," her mom pouted. "Maybe later then? We can watch *Home Alone* while we decorate."

"Sure. Sounds fun."

Tina's heart sank. She could tell under the red lipstick smile and bouffant of hair that her mother was disappointed. Still, Tina knew if she ever wanted to save enough money to buy a car that she couldn't skip a single shift at the grocery store. A new car would be her ticket to college, dating, more fun with friends, and beyond. Independence. Freedom. That's what Tina craved the most. Her mom would understand, right?

She picked up her backpack and headed down the hallway to her bedroom. The scene of the crime. The place where not so long ago, she and her two best friends summoned the demon Zozo during her Sweet Sixteen sleepover birthday party. Somehow, the residue of that night continued to linger in her rug and on her walls, in her head and in her heart. Who's big idea was it to have a sleepover anyway?

Months had passed, but she still felt paranoid and jumpy, giving a wary eye to every shadowy corner and suspicious pile of laundry. Her bedroom was a mess; though, these days, it was always a mess. Between school, work, and hanging out with friends, Tina was rarely home. Her mom was always busy at work or off romancing some new guy anyway. Even if she had time to hang out at home, she was never completely at ease in her bedroom, a side-effect of the leftover bad vibes from that cursed sleepover. Her bedroom used to be a sanctuary, a place where she could lounge around and dream, where she could act silly away from the eyes of the world. Now, home was just a stopping point between destinations. A place full of bad memories she was more than ready to leave behind.

Tina peeled off her school clothes and slipped into the unflattering, itchy uniform the grocery store made her wear. Working as a checkout girl wasn't exactly her dream job, but the video rental store wasn't hiring, and she needed to work somewhere close enough to home that she could bike to. So, Publix it was. She slicked on a fresh layer of Lip Smackers Vanilla Frosting lip gloss and smoothed her hair back into a ponytail, avoiding the gaze of her bedroom mirror for too long.

Every now and then, Tina still caught sight of a strange shadow that hovered just over her shoulder. She knew the ominous shadow was tied to the Ouija board and to Lacey, but she didn't know how or why, or where it came from. So long as she didn't look at the blob or didn't give it any attention, the shadowy mass usually went away. Like so many other things, it was a problem that Tina avoided.

Tina grabbed her backpack purse and scooted out of her bedroom as if she were being chased by a ghost. She walked toward the garage door, trying to avoid the guilt of her mother's hopeful, Christmassy gaze too.

"Bye, Mom," she called out. "I'll be home before ten."

"Is Eve picking you up?" Her mother emerged from the kitchen with a fresh batch of cookies in hand.

"Yeah, she's going to drive me home."

"Okay, great. Rick is coming over for dinner later. I can't wait for you to meet him."

"Can't wait." Tina forced a smile and hugged her mom. "Gotta go."

"Be safe out there!" Her mom called after her. "Don't forget to wear your helmet!"

"I will."

Tina entered the garage and grabbed her helmet from the handlebars of her bike. In the past, her bike was a beloved method of transportation back and forth from Lacey's house. They would ride together to the park or to the convenience store for Fruitopia drinks and sleeves of Pringles. Now, riding her bike was just a means to an end. Another relic of childhood that she was so desperate to shed. Another memory of her time with Lacey, time that she would never get back.

"Just a few more weeks of paychecks, T," she muttered to herself, strapping the helmet under her chin. "Used car, here I come."

Chapter Three

"**E**xcuse me, ma'am, could you give us a price check on this prune juice?"

Tina glanced up from her register and smiled at the familiar voice. Eve entered her checkout line, linked arm-in-arm with Deon, hauling a shopping basket full of junk food. Seeing Eve and Deon together reminded her that at least one good thing had come out of her cursed birthday sleepover. They were a cute couple, and Tina was happy for her friends, so she tried not to let her own loneliness and jealousy bubble to the surface when they were around.

"You guys can't go through my line," Tina said. "I'll get in trouble if I ring up someone I know."

"The managers don't know I'm your friend," Eve said. "Besides, we're just buying candy bars and soda. It's not like we're gonna scam you."

"*Fine*," Tina said, reluctantly ringing up their snacks. "I don't get off for three more hours. What are you doing here?"

"We're going to AMC," Eve said. "Gonna catch a movie and then come back to pick you up."

"Wait! You're not gonna go see *Scream 2* without me, are you?" Tina whined.

"I wanted to, but Deon is insisting we go see *Titanic*. We already know the boat is gonna sink. I don't know what the big deal is." Eve threw Deon a playful smirk.

"It's a romance!" Deon said. "Besides, it's historical."

"Well, let me know how it is," Tina said. "I mean, Leo is in it, so it'll probably be good."

"His hair is so fancy." Eve sighed. "Speaking of fancy hair."

Eve nodded towards the grocery store entryway. The hackles on the back of Tina's neck stood on end as Zoey and her demonic softball team entered through the automatic double doors. Zoey was dressed in Lacey's softball uniform with her blonde ponytail pulled back under a baseball cap. Chris trailed along behind her, holding her purse like a zombie butler, while a half dozen other softball uniform clad demon models skipped by her side.

"What are they doing here?" Tina moaned.

Deon snorted. "Probably buying drain cleaner to spike everyone's drinks with."

Chris grabbed a shopping cart and pushed it down the aisle. Zoey and the demon girls filled it with sports drinks and bags of chips.

"Do they even have softball games this time of year?" Tina asked.

"Probably practice for the winter league," Deon said. "Eve, let's get outta here."

Tina glanced at Eve. Her friend was still as a statue, her gaze locked in on the group of giggling, modelesque teens.

"Eve?" Tina followed Eve's gaze toward the group and her hair stood on end again. Zoey's eyes glowed, her fiery pupils locked in on Eve.

"Huh?" Eve gasped and shook her head. "Oh, sorry. Yeah, we need to go or we'll miss the movie."

"I heard *Titanic* was long," Tina said. "Are you sure you'll be done in time to get me?"

"Yeah, we're skipping the previews. Don't worry,"

Eve said. "Do you want us to stick around in case the demonites give you any trouble?"

"No. I can handle myself," Tina said. "You guys go have fun."

"If you say so." Eve sighed. "See you later."

"Okay. Bye."

Tina's pulse ratcheted up as Eve and Deon left her alone to deal with the demon horde. The truth was that she wanted her friends to stick around and back her up, but she also didn't want to ruin their date night. No. If Zoey and her crew gave her any trouble, Tina would just call the store manager and make them deal with it. Even though there were two other open lines, as if on cue, Chris wheeled the shopping cart full of sports drinks and snacks through her line. Tina steeled herself as Zoey sidled up to the register.

"Working late tonight, Tiny?" Zoey rested her elbows on the check writing platform as Tina concentrated on her work.

The mention of her childhood nickname caused Tina's blood to boil.

"You don't get to call me that," Tina said.

"Oh, don't be such a drag!" Zoey said. "Come on, why don't you join us for a night game one of these days?"

Tina snorted. "No thanks."

"Why not?" Zoey taunted. "You know you wanna play on our team."

Tina gazed up from her register at a half-dozen pairs of deadened, glowing eyes. Mallory. Janice. LaToya. Paulette. Lacey's softball team friends all looked like ultra-glam versions of their former selves. The Spice Girls on steroids with a zombie gaze.

"I said no."

"Boo." Zoey stuck out her tongue and her eyes flickered. "Your loss."

"That's gonna be $29.79."

Chris dug into his pocket and pulled out a twenty dollar bill and a ten dollar bill. He handed Tina the crisp cash in a robotic fashion, emotionless and stiff without meeting her gaze.

"Keep the change, Tiny," Zoey said. "Say 'hello' to Eve for me."

"yEaH, sAy HeLLo To eVe!" LaToya snickered, her voice high and sing-songy.

Tina clenched her jaw and held her head high as the super stylish demons grabbed their softball practice snacks. They cackled all the way out the door, laughing and screeching like teenaged harpies in their high pitched voices. Tina would be lying if she said she wasn't partially tempted to take them up on their offer. Maybe Eve was right. Maybe there was no use fighting. It would be so easy to just give in and join them to be near Lacey again. But it wasn't really Lacey. Giving in would mean losing herself, and Tina's sense of self was the one thing she knew to hold onto. Things weren't great, but Tina still knew who she was. She still had the future ahead of her, and she wasn't going to let some board game demon ruin her life too.

Tina grabbed a bottle of cleaner and sprayed her register down. She couldn't wipe away the evil residue Zoey left behind, but she could at least have a sparkling clean work station. She stared at her own mottled reflection in the stainless steel finish of the register. Something dark and smudgy hovered over her left shoulder.

"Get off!" Tina turned and swiped at her shoulder.

Nothing was there.

"Everything okay, Tina?" Lance, one of the stock clerks, entered her line. Lance was a year ahead of her in school, tall and lanky. The kind of guy who rode a skateboard and didn't seem to let much of anything bother him. His floppy, dark hair fell in his eyes as he placed a whole sub sandwich on her register.

"Yeah. I just... thought I saw something."

"So, um, do you have lunch break soon?" Lance cleared his throat. "I just got this whole sub and I'm not going to be able to finish it all."

"Oh." Tina scanned his sandwich. "I don't go on break for another hour."

"Bummer," he said. "Well, I could leave the other half for you in the break room fridge?"

Tina's stomach growled. She forgot to pack dinner. "That's really nice of you to offer."

"It's turkey and cheese with lettuce and tomato," he said. "Nothing crazy."

"Sure," Tina said. "Thanks."

"Okay, cool. I'll put your name on it so no one steals it." Lance nodded and handed her a twenty dollar bill. "Maybe we can have lunch together some other time?"

Tina handed him his change and receipt. "Yeah. Maybe."

Maybe? What was she saying? Ugh.

"Cool, cool. Catch ya later." He gave her a shy smile and grabbed his sub sandwich.

Tina cursed herself as he walked toward the break room to eat his dinner alone. Lance was a nice guy, but a co-worker with a crush was the last thing she had time or energy for. Sure, he was cute, but after what happened with Lacey, Tina didn't know if she had the heart to open up to anyone else. What if she fell for someone else and Zoey turned them into a demon too? Tina just didn't know if she could handle it.

When her lunch break rolled around, Tina went to the breakroom and found half of a turkey sub waiting for her in the fridge. The word TINA had been written on the paper bag, the "I" dotted with a heart. Tina sighed and grabbed the sandwich, grateful but hesitant. Lance was in for a big let down if he thought anything romantic could happen between them.

The rest of her shift dragged on as she scanned chicken breasts and bananas and gallons of milk for customers. After the store closed and everything was cleaned and put away, Tina waited out in front for Eve to arrive. Normally, Eve was waiting for her, but that night, her purple Dodge Neon was nowhere to be found. Tina shivered against the cold night air and pulled her hoodie tight over her uniform. After a few minutes, she scrounged a quarter from the bottom of her backpack purse and dialed the number to Eve's beeper. She punched in her code (4-1-1), followed by the number for the pay phone. It was times like these Tina wished she had her own beeper.

"Hey, are you waiting for a ride?" Lance walked out the grocery store double doors with his skateboard tucked under one arm and a Birdhouse hoodie layered over his stock clerk uniform. Off the clock, he had an even more devil-may-care look about him, a new spring in his step and a sparkle of mischief in his eye. Tina couldn't deny that he was pretty cute.

"Yeah, my friend Eve is supposed to pick me up."

"That goth girl?" Lance said. "She scares me."

Tina scoffed. "Eve would be happy to hear that."

"Not as much as that Zoey girl, though," Lance said. "Aren't you guys friends too?"

"We used to be." Tina kicked her back tire. "Not anymore though."

"She's kind of evil now, right?" Lance asked.

Tina's ears perked up. "What did you say?"

"She didn't used to be so popular and mean, right?" Lance said. "No one knew who she was before, and then all of a sudden, BAM! It was like she was the most popular girl in school. It's wild, even the seniors fall at her feet now."

"Yes!" Tina exclaimed, almost shouting. "That's

what I'm always trying to tell people!"

BRRRRINNNG!

Lance hitched his thumb toward the payphone. "That for you?"

"I hope so." Tina picked up the pay phone receiver and held it to her ear. "Hello?"

"Hey. It's me." Eve's voice crackled over the phone. "I can't pick you up tonight."

"Is everything okay?"

"Yeah. Deon and I got into an argument." The phone buzzed, electric in her ear. "Something came up."

"That's okay," Tina said.

"T?"

Tina's heart dropped to her feet. Something in the way her voice sounded chilled her to the bone. She sounded scared, not the same confident, kick-ass Eve she knew and loved. "What?"

"I really am sorry."

CLICK.

The phone buzzed its droning tone in her ear and another chill tapped at Tina's spine. Something was wrong. Beyond wrong. She turned her attention back to Lance and faked a smile to hide her worry.

"Is ... your friend not coming then?"

Tina shook her head. "No. I have to ride my bike home I guess."

"Want some company?" Lance asked. "I can ride along with you. Make sure you get home safe."

Tina sighed and stared up at the wintry night sky. Streaky clouds raced over the waning moon, making the night even darker than usual. Another bracing blast of wind licked at her back. She was in for a chilly ride home. At least she wouldn't have to do it alone.

"Sure," Tina said. "Follow me."

Chapter Four

"So then Dylan said after graduation I was gonna live in a van down by the river, in that voice you know? Everyone thought it was hilarious."

Lance let out a goofy laugh and hopped off his skateboard as they neared Tina's house later that evening. He pushed the nose of the board to the ground and popped it into the air with ease, tucking it under his arm like a football. Tina smiled and her cheeks flushed as she watched him perform the move as easily as breathing.

"He just died, you know," Tina said, her smile fading.

"Who, Dylan?"

"No. The comedian. The 'down by the river guy'. I

saw it on the news," Tina undid the clasp on her helmet. "Sorry, that's kind of a bummer."

"Yeah, total bummer. He was so funny. I love watching him on *Saturday Night Live*."

"Me too." She sighed and glanced toward her house. There was a brand new black sports car parked in the driveway, a vehicle she suspected belonged to her mom's new boyfriend. Even though she expected that he would be there, she couldn't help but be a little annoyed by the whole mom's-new-boyfriend situation.

"Well, I guess I'll be seeing you," Tina said.

"The, uh, decorations on your house look nice." Lance cleared his throat and scratched the bridge of his nose. "Are you working this weekend?"

"No. I'm supposed to be going to my dad's house for the holidays. This was my last shift until after Christmas."

"Oh, bummer."

"Yeah, I took some time off to spend with my Mom. She's probably going to be busy with her boyfriend, though."

"Oh, divorced parents. Me too. It sucks at first, but then I realized my Mom and Dad were better off separate, you know?"

Tina's cheeks grew hotter. Lance was too easy to talk to. "Exactly."

"Well, if I don't see you around, have a Merry Christmas."

Lance held out a hand. Tina gave him a crooked smile and slapped him a half low-five, half handshake.

"You too," Tina said. "See you around."

"See ya."

Lance threw her a peace sign and stepped on his board. She was disappointed that Eve didn't pick her up from work, but it had been nice to have Lance ride home with her. Tina's heart squeezed in her chest as the wheels of his skateboard *thunk thunk thunked* along the paved sidewalk. For a moment, she let her mind wander and fantasized what it might be like to have Lance as a friend. A quirky guy friend who liked the same things she did and would enter her house through her bedroom window like on *Clarissa Explains It All*. A funny skater guy friend with floppy hair who lived nearby. A guy friend who might have potential to be more than just a friend.

Another blast of winter air snapped Tina back to reality. She wasn't looking forward to meeting Rick or doing the whole happy family Christmas charade. She punched the keypad on her garage door, parked her bike and readied herself for the inevitable awkwardness of meeting Rick, TGI Friday's Regional Manager, sports car driver and exterior illumination specialist.

"Sweetie, you're home!" Tina's mom greeted her with a hug as soon as she walked in through the garage door. The house smelled like cinnamon and the remnants of some kind of baked chicken dinner. Classic Christmas music spun on the turntable and the house was aglow with multicolored lights and red and green decorations hung from every corner. Tina's frosty demeanor melted a little when she saw her childhood stocking hung on the TV console. The house looked almost exactly like it used to during Christmas time when she was a kid.

"Tina, I would like to introduce you to Rick," her Mom said. Her eyes widened and she silently mouthed the words *be nice*. "Rick, this is my daughter, Christina."

A middle-aged man in a dorky Dad sweater sporting a mustache and thick, plastic rimmed glasses rose from the couch. He walked over to Tina with his hand extended and a jovial smile on his cheeks brimming with the energy and vitality of a young Santa Claus.

"Tina! Your mom has told me all about you," he said.

Tina accepted his warm, firm handshake. As much as she wanted to hate the guy, at first glance, it was hard to. "Hi."

"I was just getting ready to leave, but I wanted to wait and meet you," he said. "Your mom made one heck of a chicken a'la king for dinner."

"You *cooked*?" Tina threw her mother a skeptical glare.

"Well, yes! I used to cook all the time before I had to take that second job," her mother said. "There's some leftovers if you're still hungry."

"I'm good. I had a sub for dinner."

"Tina, I've got to hit the road," Rick said. "It was a pleasure meeting you."

"Nice meeting you, too."

"I'm just going to walk Rick out," her mother said. "Be right back."

Tina made a beeline for the bathroom as her mother and Rick closed the front door. Once inside, she peeled off her work uniform and tried to block out the fact that her mom and Rick were probably making out in the driveway. She stepped into the shower, ready to wash the day away with a cascade of scalding water and a generous dose of Herbal Essences shampoo. After conditioning her hair and shaving, Tina emerged refreshed, reborn, and ready to face her mother and hear all about Rick.

"Tina?" her mother called.

"I'm getting dressed!"

Tina opened her dresser drawer and pulled out her only set of winter pajamas. They were usually too warm to wear any other time of the year; a pair of long sleeve flannel PJs in baby blue with a puffy white cloud print. They were her favorite, a pair she had saved up babysitting money to buy from dARiA*s. She had dreamed about buying those pajamas for months. Now, she didn't even know if she wanted to wear them. Tina shoved the trendy pajamas back into her drawer and pulled out the NO FEAR t-shirt that Lacey gave her instead.

"Are you decent?" Her mother knocked on her bedroom door.

Tina pulled the shirt over her head. "Yeah. Come in."

"So? What did you think?" Her mother sat on the edge of her bed, eyes sparkling and lips set in a smile a million miles wide. Tina had never seen her mother act this way, and didn't know whether to be happy for her or worried.

"He seems like a nice guy." Tina shrugged. "You seem to like him a lot."

"I really do." Her mother sighed dreamily. "Tina, he's asked me to go on vacation with him for the holidays."

"What?"

"I know, I know, it's sudden! His boss gave him a big Christmas bonus. He wants to take me to Colorado to go skiing. I've never been skiing before."

"Mom, I don't know if that's a good idea," Tina said.

Her mother pouted. "Why not?"

"Didn't you ever watch *Unsolved Mysteries*?" Tina plopped down on her bed. "How do you know Rick isn't a serial killer or something?"

Her mother scoffed. "Oh, that's silly."

"Or he could be like one of those guys who has a wife in every city."

"Christina!" Her mother shouted. "Please don't ruin this for me. Rick isn't like that."

"I'm just looking out for you, Mom," she said. "You don't know this guy that well."

"Yes, I do! We've been dating for three months." Her mother massaged her temples. "I know you're concerned, but please, can't you just be happy for me? Just this once?"

Tina sighed and glanced at her mother from under her mop of dripping wet bangs. She was being a jerk, and she knew it. Even though her parents had been divorced for a while now, she was still trying to get used to the idea of them moving on. Her mother deserved to have a life, and Tina wouldn't be around forever. She would be lonely when Tina left for college someday. It was good that her mom had found a friend, but it wasn't easy for her to accept.

"I'm sorry. He really does seem nice."

"So you think I should go to Colorado with him then?" Her mother lit up even brighter than the Christmas tree.

"Yeah," Tina nodded. "You'll have a blast."

"I really think I will!" Her mom clasped her hands together. "The only problem is that we need to leave Saturday night, and your Dad won't be here to pick you up until Monday."

"I'll be okay on my own for a day."

"Good." Tina's mother popped up from the bed.

"It's settled then. I'll bring you back something fabu-lous, I promise."

"You don't have to do that. Just have a good time."

"Oh, I'm going to call Rick and tell him!" Tina's mother took her face in her hands and planted a kiss on her cheek. "Goodnight, sweetie."

"Goodnight."

Tina flopped back on her bed, pondering the news that had just been laid on her. Not only was Rick dec-orating the house and coming over for dinner, now her mother was going on vacation with him. Next, they were probably going to run off and elope in Las Vegas. The thought of Rick being her step-father made her cringe. She rolled on her side and yawned, exhausted by the day. She had to be up in seven hours to start the cycle all over again. Thank goodness there was only one day left before winter break.

BRRRING!

She gasped and sat up as her see-through phone rang, cutting through her trail of thought. Even though she didn't have a beeper, Tina was lucky enough to have her own landline number and a phone in her room. Her pulse raced as she wondered who might be calling her that time of night. She had already spoken to Eve, and she didn't have many other friends who called her anymore. Tina held her breath, picked up the receiver, and held it to her ear.

"Hello?"

"Hello, Tiny." Zoey giggled in her ear. "It was so good to see you tonight!"

Tina exhaled, her heart pounding. "What do you want?"

"I have a present for you!" Zoey squealed. "A *Christmas* present."

"I don't want anything from you."

"Oh but you *love* my presents, don't you?" Zoey cackled. "Like that shirt you're wearing right now. NO FEAR, right, Tiny?"

Tina's breath hitched. "You didn't give me this shirt. My best friend Lacey did."

"Are you sure you don't want my present?" Zoey asked. "I already gave Eve her present. She loved it."

"You stay away from Eve!" Tina shouted. "And you stay away from me too!"

"Too late, Tiny."

Zoey laughed, but this time, her voice wasn't high and tinny. This time the laugh was low, a guttural growl straight from the pits of hell. The laugh echoed through the phone, shuddering the walls and rattling the fillings in Tina's teeth. Zoey's demonic presence filled the room like a dark cloud, sending a lead weight of regret straight to Tina's gut.

Tina screamed and slammed the handset on the cradle. She ended the call with so much force, the see-through phone shattered in an explosion of clear plastic, neon wires, and colorful electronics. Zoey's demonic laugh slowed through the destroyed earpiece and Tina's room was silent once more; still and quiet as the grave.

Chapter Five

Tina waited for Eve to pick her up for school the following morning, but the purple car never pulled up in the driveway. She shivered under the glow of Rick's Christmas lights, exhausted from lack of sleep and anxious with worry. Eve wasn't responding to her pages, and her mother had already left for work, so Tina only had herself to rely on. She held out until the last possible moment before strapping on her helmet and huffing it to school on her bike through the frozen December morning.

On the ride to school, she replayed her conversation with Zoey from the night before; the conversation that ended with Tina smashing her beloved clear neon phone to bits. Zoey was creepy, that was for sure, but their conversation totally freaked Tina out in a completely new and terrifying way. What had her demonic "friend" meant about giving Eve a gift? How did she know what Tina had been wearing? And what was up with the deep, wall-rattling evil laughter? The fact that Tina couldn't reach Eve only deepened her anxiety. She was eager to get to school and find out just what was going on with her friend.

Tina locked her bike up near the student parking lot just before the late bell rang. The atmosphere was light, with Christmas music echoing through the decorated hallways. Teachers and students alike were dressed in "ugly" sweaters for the last day of school, many of them wearing Santa hats or headbands shaped like reindeer antlers. Even though she was supposed to feel merry and bright, the only emotions Tina could muster up were doom and gloom.

That morning, Eve wasn't at their lockers waiting for her, and the realization that something bad may have happened gnawed a pit into Tina's stomach. The day dragged on with no signed of Eve in a torture of busy work set to the cacaphony of students gossiping about who's dating who and the upcoming Winter Break. Finally, lunch period rolled around and Tina raced to the cafeteria to find her remaining best friend. Instead, she only found a despondent looking Deon at their usual table sitting all alone. But before she could reach him, someone tugged at her backpack.

"Hey!" Tina whipped around with her hands balled into fists, ready to fight. She expected to come face-to-face with Zoey or one of her minions. Instead, she was greeted by a familiar, floppy-haired co-worker.

"Lance!" Tina gasped. "You scared the life out of me!"

"Sorry! I just wanted to stop by and say 'hey'."

"Hey." Tina glanced over his shoulder, her eyes wild as she scanned the waves of incoming students. The cafeteria was filling up, but there was no sign of Eve. No sign of Zoey. Something was *definitely* off.

"I didn't realize we have the same lunch period," Lance said, following Tina's gaze. "Are you looking for someone?"

"Yeah. My friend," Tina said. "I'm gonna go sit over there with Deon. You wanna join us?"

Lance shrugged. "Sounds cool. I'm gonna go grab lunch."

"Cool," Tina said.

Lance headed toward the lunch line while Tina searched the sea of faces in vain. When it became clear that Eve was not coming to lunch, Tina took her seat across from Deon.

"Hey." Tina took out her brown paper lunch bag.

"Hey." Deon shifted in his seat. "I saw you talking to Lance. Doesn't he work with you?"

"Yeah," Tina said. "You know him?"

Deon nodded. "We used to skate together. Are you guys dating?"

"Deon! No."

"What?"

"We're just friends," Tina said.

"You better let him know that," Deon said. "Seems like he's into you."

"Well, if he really knew me, he wouldn't be," Tina said. "Besides, I have way more important things to worry about right now. Where is Eve by the way?"

"I don't know," Deon said. "That's what I was gonna ask you. We were late for *Titanic* last night and she got mad at me. We didn't even go to the movies, she just took me home."

"I know," Tina said. "She told me."

"Well, I'm gonna need your help. I guess I messed up

with Eve somehow."

"What happened?"

"She got so mean all of a sudden." Deon rubbed the back of his neck. "I don't know. After we left the grocery store last night, it's like something snapped. She just wasn't acting like herself."

"Eve can be pretty intense sometimes," Tina said. "But she's never mean to you like that."

"Right?" Deon shook his head. "It's killing me. You know her better than anyone. Do you have any ideas? Like, maybe something is going on at home?"

"Could be. But I got a weird call from Zoey last night," Tina said, unwrapping her sandwich. "She said something about giving Eve a Christmas present."

"That's weird," Deon said.

"She said she had a present for me too," Tina said. "I don't know. Maybe Zoey was just messing with me, but I can't help but be worried with Eve being absent today. Something feels off."

"Well, she's not absent, but I think I know why she's been avoiding us." Deon's face fell as he nodded toward the cafeteria doors. "Look."

Tina pivoted in time to catch the opening act of Zoey's daily cafeteria fashion show catwalk. The usual suspects were in attendance following closely behind their pink clad queen, including a new and very familiar face. Eve slunk in at the tail of the demon horde, wearing a lilac babydoll dress, white tights, and chunky platform mary janes. Her dyed black hair was smoothed into two perfect pigtails, and her usually dark, gothic makeup was replaced with dewy pink lip gloss, peachy blush, and sparkling silver eyeshadow.

"Oh no," Tina moaned. "Not Eve!"

"Not Eve what?" Lance slid into the seat next to Tina with a tray of chicken nuggets, corn niblets, and applesauce.

"The demon squad got my girlfriend." Deon rose to his feet, his jaw clenched and lips set in a sneer. "Fuck that! I'm gonna go talk to her."

"No!" Tina grabbed the corner of Deon's jacket and sat him back down. "They'll just make you like one of them too!"

"Wait, so they're really demons?" Lance crammed a chicken nugget in his mouth.

"YES!" Tina and Deon shouted in unison.

Lance's eyes grew wide. "Heinous."

"Every day, Zoey takes another kid under her wing," Deon said. "Haven't you noticed?"

"Yeah, I mean, I just figured at first it was just a trend or whatever," Lance said, polishing off another chicken nugget. "But, dude, now that you mention it, my buddy James came to school last week looking like a model for CK One or something. And I know this sounds crazy, but his eyes were *glowing*."

"This is what we're talking about!" Tina said. "If Zoey got to Eve, then she's probably coming for us next."

"Bro, she wants to snatch everyone's souls." Deon stared at Lance, dead serious. "If we don't do something, you and me are gonna be trading in our JNCO jeans for Tommy Hilfiger."

Lance frowned. "Gross."

Tears sprung to Tina's eyes and her throat closed. It had been hard enough losing Lacey to the Ouija board demon. She had stayed strong for months, trying to live with the reality that her friend and classmates were now demons. Seeing Eve shed her personality and style and succumb to the demon virus was the last straw.

"Oh, dang. Are you crying?" Lance asked.

Tina sobbed. "I just want my friends back!"

He held out the sleeve of his flannel. "Here."

"Thanks." Tina sobbed and took the cuff of his shirt

to dry her eyes. "That's it. I'm not waiting anymore. I'm gonna do something about this. We're getting our friends back before Christmas."

"What's the plan?" Lance asked.

"We need to do an exorcism," Tina said.

"Like, with a priest or something?" Lance gave Deon a side-eye. "Do you know about this?"

Deon nodded.

"Not exactly," Tina said. "We tried to exorcise Zoey a few months back, but Ras gave us the wrong incantation or something."

"Ras?" Lance asked.

"Yeah," Deon said. "You remember Tyler?"

"Oh right," Lance nodded. "He dresses like some kind of young wizard now."

Deon snorted. "Exactly."

"Ras sucks, but we need him," Tina said. "He works at the mall. I'm going there after school to force him to help us find another demonic reversal spell. Whether he likes it or not."

"I'll go with you," Deon said. "I'll do whatever it takes to get my girlfriend back."

"There's only one problem," Tina said. "Eve is usually our ride. We can catch the bus but that takes forever."

"I can borrow my Mom's station wagon." Lance offered.

Tina and Deon exchanged skeptical glances.

"Are you sure you want to get wrapped up in this?" Tina asked.

"Yeah. I mean, I needed to go pick up a Christmas present for my Mom anyway." Lance shrugged. "Besides, if all this demon stuff is true, Zoey and her clique will come after me too. I don't wanna get my soul snatched and dress like a dork."

"Thanks." Tina laughed despite herself. "That's very cool of you."

"Yeah, thanks, dude," Deon said. "It's nice to have someone else believe us."

Tina took a bite of her sandwich even though she had no appetite. It didn't do her any good, but she couldn't help but catch glimpses of the demon squad as they ruled the cafeteria. Tina held back tears as she witnessed her two best friends laughing together through the crowd, beautiful and resplendent in their fresh fashion finds and bubblegum attitudes. Eve fit right in with the overly enthusiastic, pastel pretty group as though she had never worn dark eyeliner or listened to goth music in her life. All evidence of Eve's true personality and style had been stripped away to fit Zoey's evil homogenous catalog aesthetic.

They're still in there, Tina reminded herself.

Eve and Zoey threw their heads back and cackled to the sky. Tina's heart squeezed.

I won't give up on you, Tina promised them. *Not now. Not ever.*

Chapter Six

T he student body was rowdy and full of excitement as the dismissal bell rang, signaling the end of the school day. Friends linked arms in the hallway and obnoxiously sang along with the Christmas carols playing over the school radio. Even teachers turned a blind eye to the chaos, no doubt looking forward to two weeks of peace on Earth themselves. Tina envied their oblivious happiness. She wished she could be excited about Winter Break, but with both of her best friends now soulless fashionable demonic vessels, she could only find misery and despair.

Tina hid behind a column and waited as Zoey and Co. filled into the student parking lot. Eve was parked next to Chris's red sports car, and Tina frowned as over a dozen stylish demon teens squeezed themselves into the two vehicles. Where were they going? She shuddered at the possibility. Possession was bad enough, but Zoey was a powerful demon. Anything was possible with that many followers and that much influence.

After Zoey and her minions exited the parking lot, Tina hopped on her bike and pedaled home. She didn't know exactly what she would say to Ras, or how she would be able to trick Zoey into getting exorcised, but she would figure out those details later. For now, she needed to get home and get ready for the mall.

The brightly decorated house was empty when she pulled her bike into the garage. Lance and Deon would be there to pick her up soon, and she didn't have much time to get ready. Unlike Eve and the catalog girls, Tina didn't really know what her style was. Before the possession, Lacey had a sporty style and Eve leaned toward more gothic looks. Tina was just ... Tina. She wore what was comfortable and what fit; jeans and t-shirts mostly. Sure, she liked the clothes from dARiA*s that the catalog girls wore, but they weren't really for her. Tina didn't know *what* her style was. What did that say about her?

Her heart blipped as she searched through her closet for something to wear, and it occurred to her that she was a little nervous about seeing Lance again. Even though he had seen her at her most dorky and disheveled in her grocery store uniform, this trip to the mall felt like something else. But like she told Deon, Lance was just a friend. So why was she so worried about how she looked?

Tina popped her Veruca Salt CD in the purple boombox she got for her birthday (one good thing to come out of her Sweet Sixteen party) and scoured her closet. Looney Tunes sweater? Definitely not. Pink fuzzy crop top? Too demon girl chic. Tina finally settled on a patterned cable knit cardigan she had inherited from her grandfather. She spritzed herself with a healthy dose of Raspberry Fantasy body spray as Lance pulled up in her driveway.

"Hey, cool sweater." Lance offered a nod of approval as Tina slid into the back seat. Deon turned to give her an *I told you so* look from the front passenger seat. Nirvana's *In Utero* album played over the station wagon speakers.

"Thanks." Tina cleared her throat. "Thanks for picking me up."

"So, what are we shopping for today?" Lance asked, pulling out of the driveway.

"Revenge," Deon said. "And maybe the new Wu-Tang album. If we have time."

"I need to go to Radio Shack and get a new phone," Tina said. "I kinda smashed mine last night."

"Punk rock." Lance smirked at her in the rearview mirror. "I need to go to the candle store. My Mom loves smelly candles."

Tina giggled. "Mine too."

"But first, we gotta go find Ras," Deon said.

"How do we know he'll be there?" Lance asked.

"His mom owns the metaphysical shop," Deon said. "He works there with her. They're always there."

"I hope so."

Tina leaned back and closed her eyes as Lance drove through their town toward the mall. Her shoulders eased, and for a brief moment she was able to relax. She missed Lacey and was broken-hearted about losing Eve now too. But being with Deon and Lance made her feel safe. Like she was part of something again.

When they arrived at the mall, the parking lot was full and Lance had to circle the food court area a few times before parking way in the back. Tina shoved her hands in her pockets as she walked into the mall shoulder-to-shoulder with Lance and Deon. The thought occurred to her that maybe Ras or his mother couldn't do anything to stop the demon.

"Okay, so let's say we get Ras to help us," Tina said. "What then?"

"We do another exorcism," Deon said. "That's the whole point, right?"

"Yeah, but the demon isn't stupid," Tina said. "Last time we had to use magic handcuffs and kidnap Lacey to get her to the cemetery for the ritual."

"Whoa. Cemeteries and rituals?" Lance said. "That's cool as hell. Why didn't you lead with that? I'm so in."

"No, we can't do that again," Tina said. "Too obvious. We have to fool Zoey somehow."

Deon opened the food court door. "What about the movies? I know a guy who works at AMC. We could invite them to see *Scream 2* and set up the exorcism there. They'll be distracted watching the movie while we perform the ritual."

"What if other people come to see the movie?" Tina followed Deon into the mall. "We can't stop other people from going to the movies. I don't want anyone else to get hurt in the crosshairs."

"Good point."

A light bulb went off over Tina's head. "Oh my gosh. It's so obvious. Why didn't I think of it sooner?"

"What?" Lance asked.

"My mom is going out of town for the weekend. I have the house all to myself," Tina said. "What if I throw a Christmas party?"

"A party?" Deon asked. "With the demons?"

"Yes! I can dress up like one of the demonites and pretend I want to join them." Tina picked up her pace, reenergized. "I'll invite Zoey and Eve over to the house for a Christmas party. You guys can wait there and when they show up, we can ambush them and perform the ritual."

"That actually might work," Deon said. "Do you think Zoey will be able to tell you're lying?"

Tina shrugged. "Maybe. But I'm willing to try. I don't know what else to do."

"What day?" Deon asked. "I have to work tomorrow."

"Sunday," Tina said. "That will give me all day tomorrow to plan. Does that work for you, Lance?"

"I have to work Sunday," he said. "But the store closes early, so I can come by after I get off."

"Okay, it's settled then," Tina said. "Christmas party demon exorcism at my house."

"Sounds like a plan," Deon said. "Let's go shake an exorcism ritual out of Ras."

The three friends wandered through the mall past holiday shoppers dressed for the season. Gold and silver decorations lined every kiosk and sign in the mall, and the air was fragrant with the smell of yeasty pretzels and hot chocolate. A tiny bit of holiday cheer wriggled into Tina's heart as they passed Santa's Workshop. The line of children waiting to sit on Santa's lap and tell him their greatest wishes filled her with a sense of nostalgia. As she passed, Tina closed her eyes and threw a hail mary wish to Santa or the goddess or whoever was listening that holiday season.

Please let this work. Please help me get my friends back.

After circling the mall and dodging shoppers for twenty minutes, the Daymares and Nightdreams metaphysical shop finally came into view. It was a small boutique tucked in next to the Journey's footwear store, like a mysterious niche in some dark alleyway. The heady, sweet smell of incense hit Tina's nose before they crossed the threshold, and the trio were instantly ripped from the Christmassy mall atmosphere into a magical, mystical den. A haunting song from the Cocteau Twins wafted over the speakers, and the lighting was low. Heavy purple and black velvet drapes lined the walls and vintage tables painted black displayed metaphysical books, crystals, talismans, candles, and jewelry. Standing behind the counter at the far end of the shop was a man with long dark hair and a scraggly beard wearing all black and an expression of pure terror.

"Oh no! Not you!" Ras cowered, hiding behind the register so that only his eyes and the top of his nose were visible. "Nuh, uh! You've got to go!"

"Ras, man, chill out," Deon said.

"You're cool but the Ouija board girl can't stay," Ras said, pointing at Tina.

"What's going on out there?" A woman's voice called from behind the curtains. "Tyler, are you being rude to our customers?"

Wind chimes tinkled in the air and the black velvet curtains at the back of the store parted. Tina gasped as an ethereal older woman emerged from the back room, dressed head to toe in purple silk chiffon and lace. Her raven locks were streaked with gray and fell to her waist in loose waves, and her dark eyes were piercing and warm at the same time. Rings adorned every finger on her hands and her nails were painted a deep reddish black. She was possibly the coolest looking person Tina had ever seen. Ras's mom. The witch.

Chapter Seven

"Mom, I told you. I go by Rasputin now."

Ras rose from his hiding place and stood to his full height behind the register. He picked at the skin on his thumb and stared at his feet like a little kid who got caught doing something bad. Tina stifled a giggle as his mother gave him a *you're in trouble* look.

"I don't care if you want to change your name, but why that awful man?" The witchy woman said. "Rasputin wasn't even a real necromancer."

Ras's eyes grew wide. "*Mom*, you're embarrassing me."

"*You're* embarrassing *me* in front of customers." The woman rolled her eyes. "Welcome to Daymares and

Nightdreams. I'm Celeste. Can I help you find any-thing?"

Tina and Deon exchanged glances.

"I don't know if you have what we need," Tina said.

"I can tell this one is looking for a Christmas pre-sent," Celeste said, nodding to Lance. "Our candles are buy one, get one free. They make excellent gifts. Essen-tial for every altar."

"Oh, rad." Lance nodded. "I was gonna buy some candles today."

"Actually what we need isn't on any of your dis-plays," Tina said. "We need a demonic spell reversal. For an exorcism."

"Oh." Celeste's perfectly shaped eyebrows arched. "I'm afraid I can't help you with something like that."

"Ras gave us a spell last summer," Deon said. "It worked. Well, it almost worked."

Celeste's eyes flashed toward the register. "Were you dabbling in the dark arts again? Tyler, haven't I warned you about ..."

"Mom, it worked!" Ras interrupted. "They just per-formed the ritual wrong or something. It wasn't my fault!"

Celeste glanced toward the front of the store. A

woman in a chunky sweater with feathered bangs walked in and examined a large selenite crystal.

"Welcome to Daymares and Nightdreams!" Celeste called out, looping her arm around Tina's. "Be with you in just a minute!"

Tina gave Deon and Lance a worried look.

Celeste leaned in and whispered in Tina's ear. "Let's take this conversation in the back, shall we?"

Tina nodded.

Celeste gave her son a stern look. "Tyler, mind the store."

Ras scoffed. "But, Mom!"

"You two," Celeste said, motioning for Deon and Lance to follow her. "Come along as well."

The dark curtains parted, revealing a small room with a round table and four plush velvet dining chairs. Moons, stars and symbols were carved into the top of the lacquered round table and finished with gold paint. The room was dark, lit only by the soft candlelight of a dozen lit tapers. Tina, Deon, and Lance each took a seat at the table and the woman joined them with a very large, very old looking book.

"Is this, like, your seance room or something?" Lance asked, looking around.

"No, this is our break room," Celeste said, opening the book. "Now, explain to me exactly what kind of trouble my son got you into."

"It wasn't all his fault, ma'am," Tina said. "My friends and I were messing with stuff we shouldn't have been."

"You can call me Celeste." She smiled. "Go on."

"I was trying to impress my girlfriend Eve," Deon said. "So I asked Ras if he had a spell I could give her. I thought it was just a joke."

"I see." Celeste tsked and turned the pages of the large book. "Then what happened?"

"We recited the incantation," Tina said. "And it worked. My friend Lacey began to float and got possessed."

"That's all?"

Tina cringed. "We were also messing with a Ouija board that night."

"Let me guess; the demon Zozo?" Celeste asked.

"Yes!" Tina exclaimed. "She calls herself Zoey though. It possessed my best friend, and now the demon is possessing half the kids at school too."

"I think I understand," Celeste sighed. "My, this *is* a problem. I think that I can help you though."

"Really? Oh, that's so great." Tina breathed a sigh of relief.

"It won't be easy," Celeste said. "You'll need to trap the demon into an object and guard that object with your life."

"Does it have to be another Oujia board?" Tina asked. "She'll be suspicious if she sees one."

"No. The board never had any real power. You can use any object you wish," Celeste said. "Do you know this demon's weakness?"

Tina thought hard. "These demons are really superficial. They only care about looks. Maybe vanity is their weakness?"

Celeste nodded and took out a sheet of paper and a pen. "Use that weakness. It will help you."

Tina, Deon and Lance gave each other hopeful glances as Celeste wrote down the demon trapping instructions. After a few moments, she folded the paper in half and handed it to Tina, her lips set in a serious line.

"This incantation should work," Celeste said. "Do you have any questions?"

"Do we need to perform the ritual on holy ground?" Tina asked. "Last time we tried to do the ritual in a cemetery, but it wasn't a church cemetery. I just wonder if that's why it didn't work."

"The exorcism didn't work because my son is still learning the craft," Celeste said. "He likely gave you the wrong incantation. The location doesn't matter."

"But aren't demons, like, afraid of churches?" Deon asked.

Celeste chuckled. "This demon was channeled through a children's board game. Man-made religions have nothing to do with Zozo. This demon is older than the earth. Older than the universe. Older than time. As I said, location doesn't matter. What matters is intention, and performing the ritual with love. You must be brave, you must be smart, and most of all, you must have heart if you want to release your friends."

Tina sighed. She wasn't brave *or* smart. But she did love her friends. "Okay. I'll give it a try."

"Wait, wait, wait," Deon said. "I don't think it's gonna be that easy. This demon is smart. What do we do if it tries to trick us again?"

Celeste nodded. "You're right to be cautious. This demon loves to play games."

"That's true," Tina said. "The demon is an expert at mind control. Zoey loves to play with everyone's head."

"The demon most likely achieves this mind control through repetition," Celeste explained. "Chanting, copying, or doing the same thing over and over again."

"That explains why she's making everyone look like fashion copycats," Tina scoffed. "So how do we fight it then?"

"Just like with the demon's weakness, you must learn to read their expressions and actions," Celeste said. "If you discover that they are repeating something, you must find a way to break that repetition."

"Sounds confusing," Tina said. "We'll do our best though."

"You must also perform the ritual exactly as the instructions say or it won't work," Celeste warned. "It's almost the winter solstice, a powerful night for magic when portals to other dimensions are open and the veil between worlds is at its thinnest."

"Winter Solstice," Lance said. "Rad."

Celeste gave Lance a side-eyed glare and continued. "Repetition is also key to binding this demon to another object. Recite this incantation before midnight on the solstice and you will have the best chance at success."

"Like last time," Deon said.

"Right," Tina nodded. "Celeste, thank you so much.

We really appreciate your help."

"I'm sorry that my son misguided you," Celeste said. "Dabbling in the dark arts is no joke. Hopefully next time you'll be more careful."

"We will."

Tina tucked the instructions in her jeans pocket and Celeste led them back out onto the store room floor. Lance bought two candles in sandalwood and clove fragrances before they left. Tina and Deon browsed the rest of the store while Ras rang up the purchases. As they left the store with their goods in hand, Celeste called after them.

"Good luck," she said. "Come back and let me know how it went. And don't forget, candles are always buy one, get one free!"

"Man, I wish they had see-through phones in stock."

Tina examined her new black portable phone from Radio Shack as they drove home from the mall later that afternoon. Lance's shopping bag of candles sat next to her in the back seat, clinking together with every bump in the road. Deon's new Wu-Tang album played over the station wagon stereo.

"So, do you think the exorcism will really work this time?" Deon asked.

Tina shrugged and shook her head. "It has to."

"Tyler's mom seemed nice," Lance said. "I hope my mom likes those candles."

"Focus, Lance! We need to think of an object to trap the demon in again," Tina said. "Celeste said we need to use something that appeals to their weakness."

"Hey man, can you drop me off at Cool Flix?" Deon asked. "I need to check my schedule and make sure I'm off Sunday night so I can help with the exorcism."

Another light bulb went off over Tina's head. "Cool Flix! Perfect!"

"What?" Deon asked. "We can't trap Zozo in the video store."

"No! But we can trap the demon in a VHS tape!" Tina said. "It's perfect. She won't be able to resist filming herself."

"Ohhhh," Deon said. "So, like, we can record her with a camcorder and that will trap Zozo in the VHS?"

"Something like that," Tina said. "You've heard of cursed VHS tapes before, right? The legend had to have come from somewhere."

"Do you have a camcorder?" Deon asked.

"No." Tina frowned. "I guess I could buy one. They're so expensive."

"I have one," Lance said. "I can bring it to your place after I get off work."

"Really?" Tina asked. "You have a camcorder?"

"Yeah. My friends and I use it to film our skate tricks," he said. "Once we have some good footage we're gonna send in a tape to Thrasher."

"Wow, Lance. I had no idea you were so enterprising." Deon laughed.

"Hey, man, laugh it up. Skateboarding is a multi-million dollar enterprise," Lance said. "I just need some sponsors and then I can try to qualify for the X-Games."

"That's actually very cool of you, Lance," Tina said. "I'd love to see you skate some day."

Tina blinked as the words crossed her lips. What was she saying? Tina wasn't some sideline girl who watched boys play sports. What was happening?

Lance pulled into her driveway as the sun was beginning to set. Her house was aglow with multicolor Christmas lights, and even though there was still plenty to worry about, Tina had a shred of hope and a plan. She leaned down over the driver's side window to face Lance and Deon and tell them goodbye.

"So, I'll see you guys Sunday then?"

"Yep," Deon said. "I'll be there. I can bring a couple of blank VHS tapes."

"Perfect."

"Me too," Lance said. "I'll bring the camcorder."

Tina sighed. "I really hope this works."

"Can I have your number?" Lance asked. "You know, just to make sure you still want me to come over on Sunday and all."

"Yeah, sure." Tina pulled a pen out of her backpack purse. "Good thing I picked up a new phone today. This is my direct line."

Lance held his hand out to her. Her heart fluttered as she grabbed his wrist and wrote her phone number on his palm in purple ink.

"Don't wash your hands," she said. "See you guys."

"See ya," Lance said.

Tina stood in her driveway and waved as Lance backed his mother's station wagon out. A chilling breeze whipped through the neighborhood, causing her hair to fly around her head like a halo. A waning quarter moon hung hazy in the early evening sky as the darkest night of the year edged nearer. The winter solstice was nearly upon them, the portal to kick Zozo back to demon land would be wide open, and Tina would be ready to fight.

Chapter Eight

Tina awoke the following morning to the fragrant aroma of cinnamon and vanilla and a sinking sensation in her gut. She groaned and turned over in her bed, wincing against the sunlight that streamed in through her blinds. It was the first day of winter break, and she should have been excited. She should have slept in. But Tina had no time to be lazy. She had a party to throw and a demon to exorcise.

"Good morning, sleepyhead!"

Tina's mother greeted her brightly as she padded out to the kitchen. Her mother was already dressed for the day in a neon pink track suit with a bright green turtleneck layered underneath. A suitcase was packed and waiting by the front door.

"Hungry?" She asked. "I've got cinnamon rolls."

"Starving." Tina yawned. "What time are you leaving today?"

"Rick is going to pick me up in about fifteen minutes," she said. "I'm going to leave some cash for you on the counter so you can order pizza if you want."

"Thanks."

Tina hadn't meant to answer so flatly. Even though her plan to exorcise the demon from her best friend was contingent on her mother leaving, Tina still felt weird about it. Sure, her mother deserved to have a little fun, but it was Christmas break after all. She had taken off time from work to spend with her mother, and now she was leaving town with her new boyfriend instead. The whole situation rubbed her the wrong way.

"I also left a phone number for the ski lodge where we'll be staying." Her mother frowned. "Tina, are you sure you're okay with this?

"Huh?" Tina shook her head and forced a smile. "Yeah, fine. Why?"

"I wouldn't blame you for being a little upset that I'm leaving." Her mother plated up a large cinnamon roll and pushed it toward Tina. "We were supposed to spend the weekend together."

"It's okay, Mom," Tina said. "You deserve to get away. Besides, Rick seems nice."

"He really is." Her mother smiled, eyes sparkling and rosy cheeked. "Okay, I have to finish getting ready!"

"Tank fa da cinnama roll," Tina said, her mouth full of pastry.

Tina glanced at the clock over the kitchen sink. It was already after nine a.m. She needed to get a shower and plan her visit to Lacey/Zoey. If she wasn't careful, Zoey would snatch her soul before she had a chance to put her plan in action. Tina knew she needed to do something to convince Zoey to come to a Christmas party, and to trick her into thinking that Tina truly wanted to join her horde of demonic teens. The only problem was, Tina didn't know how.

The doorbell rang as Tina helped herself to a second cinnamon roll. Her mother ran to the door as though she was a teenager herself. When she opened the door, Rick was waiting on the other side dressed in an identical tracksuit, only his was blue.

"Ready to hit the slopes?"

"Ready as I'll ever be!" Tina's mom handed him her luggage, then swooped back into the kitchen. She planted a magenta lipstick kiss on Tina's cheek and wrapped her in an Exclamation! perfumed hug. "I'm going to miss you. I love you so much."

"Love you too, Mom," Tina said. "Bye, Rick."

"Thanks for letting me borrow your Mom, kiddo," Rick said. "Maybe we can all go on vacation for your spring break. Have you ever been on a cruise before, Christina?"

"A cruise!" Her mother squealed. "Oh, wouldn't that be fun!"

"Yeah. Sure," Tina said, trying not to cringe. If Rick was on the fast track to being her new step-dad she was going to have to make nice. He was kind of a goober, but seemed to be a good enough guy. Besides, a cruise might not be so terrible either. Tina took a deep breath and hoped that Rick hadn't been featured on a past episode of *America's Most Wanted*. "Have a safe trip."

"I'll call you when we land!" Her mother waved and blew a kiss. "Merry Christmas!"

"Merry Christmas to you."

The door closed and Tina listened as Rick's black sports car *vroomed* to life. The scent of cinnamon rolls hung heavy in the air, her house echoey as a tomb now that she was all alone. The Christmas decorations that her mother had so lovingly hung leered at her, plastic eyes watching from every fake Santa, reindeer and angel.

"It's just us now, guys." Tina said. "Time to get this show on the road."

It had been a long time since Tina had bothered to do her hair and makeup. She could never get her bangs to stay just right, and her eyeshadow application was always wonky. Still, she needed to make a big impression on Zoey if she was going to lure the demon to her Christmas party. She needed to prove that she wanted to be one of her demonic squad.

What she needed was a makeover.

Tina retreated to the en suite bathroom in her bedroom and opened the cabinet doors under the sink. Her caboodle full of makeup had been collecting dust for months, as well as the box of R57 Cherry Bomb hair dye she bought at the beginning of summer. Tina wanted to dye her hair to look like Angela's in *My So-Called Life* but was always too chicken. Now, in need of a total transformation, Tina knew that the box of semi-permanent dye was going to be her best bet. She draped an old towel over her shoulders, read the instructions on the box, and applied the bright red colored goo to her hair and scalp.

An hour later, Tina emerged from the bathroom with cranberry colored hair that shone like the sea. In the light, her hair glowed almost neon magenta, and that was fine with Tina. The demon squad seemed to love ultra-feminine styles, and so Tina would base her costume look around a pretty-in-pink aesthetic. She grabbed a handful of multicolored mini butterfly clips from the depths of her Caboodle and stared into the mirror, trying to figure out how to do the twisted look. She pulled her bangs away from her face in rows and secured the twists to her crown with the clips. Her hairstyle looked a little wonky, but it would do.

Tina rummaged through her closet and discovered a pink floral dress that her mother had bought her for Easter a few years back. The dress was a little shorter on her now, but with a pair of tights, it would look like a babydoll dress. She topped off the look with a fuzzy pink cropped sweater and a pair of black slip-on platform sandals, the only high heels she had. Satisfied with her outfit, Tina dug into the caboodle.

"A-ha!" She smirked and uncovered a small pot of silver glitter goo. "Perfect."

She swiped the silver glitter goo on her eyelids, followed by a dusting of peach blush. She outlined her lips with brown lip liner and filled them in with a rusty red matte lipstick. Finally, Tina finished her look with a swipe of Dr. Pepper lip gloss and stood back to appraise her makeover.

"Holy crap," she whispered. "I look just like one of them."

Just then, the doorbell rang and Tina nearly jumped out of her skin. She wasn't expecting anyone, and the prospect of an uninvited demonic guest would ruin her plan. Her heart slammed in her chest as Tina realized that she was all alone, with no home security system, no guard dog. No one to hear her scream. No one to save her.

She tiptoed to the front door, peered through the peephole and let out a sigh of relief.

"Lance!" She opened the door, stunned. "What are you doing here?"

"Whoa." Lance stared back at her, his jaw hung wide open. He was dressed in his stock clerk uniform with his skateboard tucked under his arm. In his hand was the sweater she had worn to the mall the day before. "I … you left this in my mom's car yesterday. I just wanted to bring this back to you."

"Thanks." Tina took her cardigan from him and tucked a lock of burgundy hair behind her ear. "Are you heading to work?"

"Yeah." He cleared his throat. "You look good. I mean, different. I mean, I like what you did to your hair."

"It's dumb," Tina said. "I'm getting ready to go over to Lacey's—I mean, Zoey's—house. I needed to make myself look like them so they'll think I want to join their demon squad."

"Oh, right. Rad. Good plan."

"Her place is on the way to work," Tina said. "Wanna ride together?"

Lance nodded. "Yeah. Cool."

"One sec. I just need to lock up."

Tina's pulse was still racing as she grabbed her house keys and backpack purse. She caught her new reflection in the kitchen window, barely recognizing the red-haired girl who stared back at her. Over her shoulder, a dark mass wavered. She held its smokey gaze for a moment, daring it to move or float away. Instead, the ominous blob stayed with her, hovering nearby like a dripping, creepy rain cloud.

"Not today," she said. "Go away."

Tina flipped off the kitchen light and her reflection disappeared.

Chapter Nine

"And then I cried so much, my mom had to take me to the emergency room." Lance hopped off his skateboard. "Turns out I just had Nintendo thumb."

"Wait, that's a real thing?" Tina's tires screeched to a halt.

"Yeah. I had to take ibuprofen and wear a wrist wrap for a few days," he said. "I was banned from playing Mortal Kombat 3 for like, a month."

"Wow." Tina laughed. "Sorry to hear that."

"It's okay. I ended up really getting into skateboarding when I had to take a break from gaming, so it all worked out."

Tina sighed and glanced at the sky. "I miss being a kid sometimes when stuff like not being able to play video games was my biggest problem."

"I heard that," Lance said. "Best friend demons aren't, like, a normal teenage problem though, you know?"

Tina scoffed. "For real."

"It's cool that you're doing something about it though," he said. "I think most people would give up. My friends wouldn't put their neck out like that for me."

"I'm actually pretty terrified," Tina admitted. "I'm afraid I'll freeze up or screw up again. I'm afraid that I'll become like them."

"I get it. It's not the same thing, but that's how I felt before I began doing skate tricks. Like, what if I fall, what if I get hurt," he said. "But you push through the fear if it's something you really want."

"Fear makes me freeze up," Tina said. "But I was too scared to fight back before and things only got worse. I can't just keep sitting back while everything falls apart."

Lance nodded at the grocery store. "I gotta go or I'll be late for my shift."

"Okay. Thanks for bringing me my sweater," Tina

said. "See you at the party tomorrow night?"

"You know it."

Lance extended a closed fist toward her. Tina bumped his fist with her knuckles. They both splayed their hands and made an explosion sound at the same time.

"You're pretty rad, Tina," Lance said.

"Me?" Tina hugged her arms to her chest. "No, I'm pretty boring, actually."

"You could never be boring," he said. "Catch ya tomorrow?"

"Totally." Tina smiled.

"Peace out!" Lance held up to fingers, winked and disappeared into the store.

Tina's cheeks were on fire as she pulled out of the parking lot and set off toward Lacey's house. Being around Lance made her feel anxious, goofy and self-conscious all at once, feelings she knew well. In fact, this heart-racing, flushed face sensation was how she used to feel around Lacey all the time once eighth grade rolled around. Well, all the time before Zozo snatched her body and soul. Tina had struggled with the fact that she crushed hard on Lacey and struggled even more when she became possessed. But now, this thing with

Lance was confusing her all over again. Did she also like boys or just Lance? Either way, she didn't have time to ponder the details of her non-existent romantic life. Tina had a demon to exorcise.

The Dennison house was decorated to the nines when she arrived a few moments later, with twinkly lights lining every inch of roof. Even in the daytime, Tina was impressed with the amount of decor that Lacey's parents had installed. The house looked every bit as cheerful as all of the other single-family, suburban homes on the block. However, something sinister lurked behind the giant plastic Santa and the ornate front door wreath. Something Tina and her friends had accidentally unleashed.

Tina parked her bike in front of the garage, straightened her skirt, and knocked on the front door. A few moments later, Lacey's mother, Mrs. Dennison answered the door wearing a white marabou trimmed silk nightgown. Her face and neck were flushed and she held a red and green martini glass sloshing full of ice and clear liquid.

"Tina! Why, I barely reckanize you!" Mrs. Dennison exclaimed, her voice slurred. "Won you come in? Eve is already here."

"Eve?"

Tina's knees turned to jelly. She had already anticipated how difficult it would be to face Zoey on her own, but she hadn't accounted for anyone else to be there too. Would she be able to fend off two of her demonic former friends? Would she be able to reign in her emotions and keep focused on the task at hand? The fact that they were hanging out without her would have hurt her feelings at the beginning of summer. Now that they were possessed by fashion demons, Eve and Zoey hanging out alone felt more like a threat.

"Well don juss stand out there, silly! Iz nearly fifty degrees ousside!" Mrs. Dennison hiccuped. "You'll catch a chill."

Tina crossed the threshold into the Dennison home for the first time in months. Just like her house, every square inch was plastered in tinsel, garland, and holly. An old-fashioned black and white Christmas movie played on the big screen TV as Mrs. Dennison plopped down on their overstuffed green leather couch.

"They're back in Lacey's room," Mrs. Dennison said. "You ghouls have fun."

Ghouls. Mrs. Dennison's drunken slur was spot-on.

Tina held her breath and walked down the hallway

that she had traveled so many times before. Lacey's framed family photos smiled down at her from the drywall as she ascended upon the demon's lair. With every step, Tina saw her friend age year by year, her childhood images frozen behind wood and glass. At the beginning of the hallway was a framed kindergarten photo of Lacey, her smile missing front teeth and blonde hair pulled into two pigtails. Her elementary and middle school portraits all staggered behind, showing her friend grow more and more lovely with each passing year. Family vacation photos. Softball photos. Finally, she reached Lacey's tenth grade fall portrait, or rather, Zoey's portrait. She looked different here. The light was gone from her eyes and her teeth were whiter. Sharper. Her hair was shinier, her smile more sinister. The portrait didn't show the Lacey that Tina knew and loved.

When she reached Lacey's bedroom door, Tina didn't bother to knock. She didn't care about violating the demon Zoey's privacy. She needed the element of surprise on her side. Tina exhaled, and before she even entered the room, the smell of sparkling raspberry and brimstone hit her nose. She held her breath again, turned the knob, and opened the door to Lacey's room.

Tina's guts instantly sank to the floor as she spied her

two best friends. Zoey and Eve were seated at the mirrored vanity, makeup, nail polish, and hairspray scattered all over the counter. Tina's eyes met the gaze of her demonic friends — four glowing pupils staring back at her. Only, in their reflection, Zoey and Eve weren't the beautiful catalog models that she knew them to be. In their reflection, their skin was sallow and hung from bony protrusions in their cheeks. Their teeth were yellow and jagged, and their nails long, cracked, blackened daggers. What little hair they had hung in patchy wisps from mottled, scab-riddled scalps. The mirror showed the demons' true reflections, and the realization brought a scream to Tina's lips.

Zoey and Eve smiled wide, demonic grins in the mirror. Then, in tandem, their heads turned to the left. And turned. And turned. And turned until their heads were completely facing backwards, their horrible, glowing eyes piercing right into Tina's soul.

"Well, if it isn't our little Tiny Tina," Zoey cackled.

"Looks like *someone* got a makeover," Eve trilled.

Tina sucked in a shuddered breath as she attempted to regain her composure.

"Hello, Zoey. Eve."

"Come to play dress up with us?" Zoey asked. "I have

a demon who would just love to try on your skin."

"That's why I'm here," Tina said, the words sounding forced and foreign in her mouth.

"I knew you would finally come around." Zoey stood and spun her head around so it sat straight on her neck again. Eve followed suit and the two demons crossed the room toward Tina. When they turned away from the mirror, Zoey and Eve didn't appear to be gaunt and hideous. Even though their reflections showed their true, ghoulish nature, to the naked eye, the teens appeared as the clear-skinned beauties Tina knew them to be.

"It won't hurt." Zoey stroked a lock of Tina's freshly dyed hair. "Well, maybe just a little."

"I want to join you," Tina said, mustering up the last bit of courage she had. "But not here. At my house."

"Why not now?" Eve purred. "It would be so easy. Just like falling asleep."

"My mom is out of town," Tina said. "I have the house to myself. I want to have one more party, like old times. A Christmas party, just for us. We can have snacks and hang out. No Ouija boards."

Zoey appraised Tina, her gaze scanning up and down from her trendy footwear to her glittery eyeshadow.

Tina momentarily flashed back to the time she and Eve spent trapped in the fashion catalog and how hypnotizing it all had been. In Zoey's demonic fashion world, everyone was beautiful. Under the demon's spell, Tina could have everything she ever wanted and more. Popularity. Good looks. Fashionable clothes. Fun times. But underneath it all, she would be rotten, just like them. No, she had to resist. She was only there to pretend.

"Well, she certainly looks the part," Zoey said, locking her gaze with Tina's. "How do we know that you're sincere?"

"I think we should just turn her now," Eve said. "She can't be trusted."

"I miss you," Tina said. "I miss us all being friends. I just want to be cool like you. I want us all to be able to hang out again."

Zoey and Eve exchange evil glances.

"I can also invite Deon to our Christmas party," Tina suggested. "Then you can turn him. Eve, I know he misses you too."

Eve's perfectly plucked eyebrows twitched. For a moment, Tina thought that she could sense a glimmer of her friend just below the surface. Perhaps the demons weren't completely in control after all.

"We *do* need more delicious boys." Eve mused, flicking her gaze to Zoey. "They're so good for heavy lifting and holding things. Zozo, too bad your boyfriend is nothing more than a brainless coat rack."

"At least he has a car," Zoey said. "What can Deon do for me?"

"He has a karaoke machine," Tina said. "I can tell him to bring it to the party."

"Oh, I love karaoke!" Zoey shrieked, bouncing up and down. "It's settled then. We'll come to your house tonight."

"Tomorrow," Tina said. "I can't tonight."

The demon's eyes grew dark, its voice deeper. "No. Tonight."

"Deon has to work tonight. He won't be able to bring the karaoke machine until tomorrow," Tina said. "Please, just give me one more day. I won't put up a fight. We'll have a good time."

"Fine." Zoey's lips spread into a big, fake smile. "Be sure to have lots of good snacks. And movies."

"I will," Tina said. "See you both tomorrow. My house. After dark."

Zoey and Eve returned to the vanity, immediately inspecting their reflections. The longer they stared at themselves, the more ghoulish they became. As Tina let herself out of the room, Zoey called out to her one last time.

"See you tomorrow, Tiny. It's gonna be a Christmas party to die for."

Chapter Ten

"**I** can't believe I'm having another party."

Tina pushed her shopping cart through the aisles of the grocery store the following morning with Deon at her side. She had a shopping list in hand, a stomach full of bees, and five crisp twenty dollar bills her mother left for groceries. Tina intended to use every last cent for party supplies, starting with buy one, get one free bags of chips.

"How much stuff do we need to get?" Deon asked. "Do demons even eat?"

"Oh yeah. They love junk food," Tina said. "They're still in teenage bodies after all."

"True." Deon grabbed a case of Dr. Pepper.

"Oh no, get the store brand stuff," Tina said. "I've only got a hundred bucks to spend."

"You know how Zoey is," Deon said. "If you don't have the brand name stuff, her head will spin."

"Literally." Tina sighed. "You're right. Let's get it."

"Did someone say 'snacks'?"

Two gangly arms encircled Tina and Deon into a group hug. Tina smiled and looked up at Lance, dressed for his shift in his stock clerk uniform.

"Aren't you supposed to be on the clock?" She playfully elbowed him in the ribs.

"Yeah, I'm on in five minutes," he said.

"Still good to come over tonight?" Deon asked.

"Definitely. I wouldn't miss a real life exorcism." Lance smirked and wiggled his eyebrows at Tina. "Save some of those snacks for me."

"I'll try," Tina said. "Are you going to bring the camcorder?"

"Definitely. I get off at ten. I'll go home after and pick it up, then bring it to your place."

"Please don't forget," Tina said. "We can't trap the exorcised demon without it."

"Demon, or demons?" Deon asked. "If Eve is possessed too, doesn't she need her own VHS tape?"

"Oh crap." Tina said. "I didn't think about that. I don't really know how all this works."

"Maybe if you exorcise the main demon, then the rest of them follow suit," Lance said. "You know, like in *The Lost Boys*, how you have to kill the head vampire?"

"Makes sense," Tina said. "Celeste's instructions made it seem like we only needed to worry about trapping the main demon."

"Good," Deon said. "I can't stand to think about a demon taking up residence in my girlfriend's skin for another minute. This has to end. *Tonight*."

"Well the time clock is calling my name. Gotta go punch in," Lance threw up a peace sign. "Catch you all on the flip."

"Later."

Tina smiled to herself and glanced at the shopping list.

Deon cleared his throat. "So, still don't think Lance is into you?"

"Doesn't matter," Tina said. "Lacey and Eve need us. We have to focus."

"Alright, alright." Deon sighed. "What else do we need to get?"

Tina turned into the spice aisle. She scanned the

shelves, her gaze landing on a row of cylinder containers. She picked up two of the containers and showed them to Deon.

"Salt. Lots of it."

"Right." Deon grabbed two more containers. "Probably need more. Just to be safe."

"I've never had a Christmas party before," Tina mused. "What are we even supposed to do?"

"Does it matter?" Deon asked. "The point is to lure them in and trap their demon asses."

"Well, we have to be able to keep them entertained until midnight," Tina said. "I guess the karaoke machine will be a good enough distraction. That reminds me, did you get the VHS tapes?"

"Yep. I got a whole stack just in case," he said.

"Thank you for helping me," Tina said. "You know, I couldn't do this without you."

"Are you kidding? I'm gonna fight for my girl," Deon said. "I already feel guilty that they sucked her in. That night, when we were supposed to see *Titanic*? I knew something was wrong then. I could have stopped her."

"D, this is *not* your fault," Tina said. "No one can stop Zoey."

Deon frowned. "That's what I'm worried about."

Tina pushed her shopping cart into the register line and a sinking sensation wormed into her chest. What if she was right? What if the incantation that Celeste gave her didn't work? What if they performed the ritual wrong again? Either way, it was too late now. She laid her party snacks on the register and made a second silent Christmas wish to Santa, the Goddess, whoever was listening.

Please, please. Let this work.

She needed to do whatever it would take to get her friends back. She had to be brave. She had to be smart. If she failed, then there was no telling what Zoey would do, or what would become of her. She had to do everything right this time. She had to.

"Where should I put this?"

Deon arrived at Tina's house later that afternoon wheeling an enormous karaoke machine on a dolly through her front door. The kitchen counter was laid out with chips and cookies, and two frozen pizzas were baking in the oven. The fridge was stuffed with canned sodas, jars of salsa, and gallons of fruit punch. Christmas music played softly from her purple boombox and the house was spotless and festively decorated for the holiday. Tina had even dressed for the occasion in a pair of white jeans and a green and red sweater. Everything was perfect, and under any other circumstance, Tina would be bubbling with Christmas excitement and cheer. However, on that night, the eve of the winter solstice, the night where she had one chance to make everything right, Tina only felt dread.

"Set up the karaoke machine over there, next to the tree," Tina said. "I moved the love seat into my mom's office to make room."

Deon wiped his brow, sweating despite the chilly evening air. Unlike Tina, he was not dressed in Christmas attire, opting instead for his usual goth uniform of wide-leg black jeans and a Skinny Puppy t-shirt layered over a long-sleeve mesh top.

"Do you have electrical outlets over here?" he asked.

"Yeah," Tina said. "You can use the same one that the tree is plugged into."

Deon brought the equipment to the corner of the living room and got to work setting up cables. The karaoke machine was massive, a giant box with a TV screen attached to it and more dials and lights than Tina knew what to do with. Deon also had a sound board that acted as a DJ booth, which took up much of the back wall near the Christmas tree. Tina had already rolled up the area rug in anticipation of the big event and made a large pentagram on the floor with black electrical tape.

"We have to position the microphone stand in the center of the star," Tina said. "Once we roll the rug back over it, no one should be able to notice."

"What time is everyone getting here?" Deon asked.

"I dunno, like around seven or eight?" Tina said.

"Got the incantation memorized?" Deon asked.

"Yep." Tina pushed her sleeve up and displayed her forearm. "I wrote it all down here too, just in case."

"What about the salt?"

Tina nodded. "Strategically stashed around the house."

"I brought the blank VHS tapes," he said. "Where do you want them?"

"I guess stack them on top of the TV stand," Tina said. "I sure hope Lance gets here with the camcorder in time."

"Time is something we don't have," Deon said. "Here, help me set up the microphone."

Tina and Deon worked together to roll the carpet out, covering the giant pentagram. She mentally noted where the center of the star would be and placed the microphone stand on top of the carpet. Deon flipped on the screen attached to the huge, boxy machine and brought a microphone to his lips.

"Testing, one, two." His voice echoed through the speakers. "Cool. It works."

"You gonna start us off with a song?" Tina asked.

"I'm too nervous to sing anything tonight," Deon said. "I need to chill."

"Yeah, you look kinda sweaty," Tina said. "It's gonna work this time."

"It better. I don't know what I'll do if I can't help Eve." Deon grabbed a stool and sat at the kitchen counter. "So, what's the plan?"

"Keep stuffing their faces with snacks and let them go wild on the karaoke machine until Lance gets here." Tina pulled the paper from her jeans pocket. "Then, when he gets here, we can turn on the camcorder and get things rolling. We have to wait until it's almost midnight to recite this incantation anyway."

Tina glanced down at the paper, reading the words that she had gone over a hundred times since Friday. The incantation was written in a strange language similar to the one that Ras had given her last summer. Celeste's elegant handwriting seemed to shimmer off the page, as if backlit somehow. She pushed her sleeve up. The words on her arm were glowing too.

"Whoa. Check it out."

"Why is it glowing like that?" Deon asked.

"I don't know. Maybe it's because the magical thinning of the veil time is near or whatever." Tina shrugged. "I don't remember Ras's dud incantation glowing when we tried to do this before. Maybe it means our exorcism will work this time."

"I hope so. I hope these demons get exactly what they deserve."

DING DONG!

Tina and Deon exchanged glances. The cackling laughter of demonic creatures wafted in through the door over the Christmas music playing on Tina's boombox. The doorbell rang again and heavy fists pounded on the front door in a thunderous wave.

"Let us in, Tiny!" Zoey said. "We know you're in there!"

Tina sighed and straightened her shoulders. "Here goes nothing."

Deon took his place behind the karaoke sound board, his usually calm and collected features pinched in a blend of anger and fear. Tina grasped the knob, opened the door, and gasped. Lacey and Eve stood in the darkened doorway of her home, their ghoulishly beautiful features illuminated in the multicolored Christmas lights. Behind her two best friends, two dozen kids from school lined up, waiting to come in.

"Well, aren't you going to let us in?" Zoey said.

"What... Why are they all here?" Tina stammered.

Panic gurgled in her throat, a burning wave of hot acid. Bodies pushed past Tina and her knees nearly buckled beneath her. Eve and Zoey stood at the door, ushering both regular teenagers and demonic, glowing-eyed kids into her home one-by-one. Out on the street, a dozen cars pulled up, each overflowing with festively-clad teenagers.

"It's a party, right?" Zoey cackled. "So let's *party*!"

Chapter Eleven

"**I** can't believe Zoey invited the entire 10th grade."

Tina cowered behind the DJ booth next to Deon as her living room filled with rowdy teens. Demonic teenagers and regular teenagers alike filled every square inch of the house, dressed to the nines and ready to party. Someone had brought in two cases of Zima, and another person had switched out the Christmas music on Tina's boom box for Cypress Hill. Her quiet Christmas party/DIY exorcism had turned into a full-on high school holiday rager.

"Surprised they didn't bring a keg," Tina said. "Where would you even get a keg of beer from?"

"Beats me. Keg beer is too cliche," Deon said. "You know Zoey would tell them to bring something trendy to drink."

"True," Tina moaned. "If I live through this night, my mother is going to kill me."

"Sorry, dude," Deon said. "You know, house parties aren't nearly as fun as the movies make them look."

"Especially when half of the guests are literal demons." Tina made a gagging sound. "Oh no. I think that kid is gonna throw up on my mom's Santa rug."

Sure enough, Marquise Johnson clutched his stomach and barfed a stream of grain alcohol onto the floor. His friend Gordon grabbed a decorative Christmas dish towel to clean it up. All around them, teenagers were making out, standing on her dining room table, and chugging Zima, wine coolers, and Dr. Pepper like their lives depended on it.

"Great," Tina said. "Just perfect."

"Should we call the cops?" Deon asked. "I know we had planned to do this exorcism thing, but this is getting out of control."

"No way," Tina said. "I'll just get in trouble, and everyone will still be possessed."

"Good point." Deon nodded in agreement. "We've

got bigger problems anyway. Where's Eve and Zoey? I haven't seen them in a while."

"Looking for us?" Zoey emerged from Tina's bedroom dressed in a familiar NO FEAR shirt. It was, of course, the t-shirt Lacey had gifted to Tina for her Sweet Sixteen, only Zoey had modified the shirt, blocking the "NO" out with black permanent marker and cutting the oversized, boxy tee into a sexy crop top.

"My shirt!" Tina gasped.

"*My* shirt now." Zoey snapped her fingers. Her boyfriend appeared from behind her, rigid and zombie-like. "Chris, go find us something fun to sing on the karaoke machine."

"I'm DJ-ing on karaoke tonight," Deon said.

"Fat chance," Zoey cackled. "I know you and Tiny are up to something. But don't worry, I'm in charge now. Tonight's gonna be a scream!"

Chris's eyes glowed as he mashed buttons on the karaoke machine. The lyrics for Mariah Carey's *All I Want for Christmas is You* queued up on the screen.

"Ahhhh, I love this song!" Zoey screeched.

Eve grabbed a microphone and handed it to Zoey.

Tina and Deon glanced at each other and covered their ears.

The entire party stopped to watch as Zoey laid into the pop Christmas ballad. Even though the demon knew every lyric by heart, the song still sounded screechy and awful. Zoey's voice was as melodic as a cat stuck in a dryer spinning on high heat. When the song was finished, all of the party guests cheered and clapped. Zoey curtseyed and handed the microphone to Eve.

"Your turn!"

Chris queued up *All I Want for Christmas is You.* Again.

Eve's eyes glowed as she brought the microphone to her lips and laid into the pop Christmas ballad. The formerly rowdy teens continued to pay attention to the karaoke performance, swaying together in unison. Thankfully, Eve was a better performer than Zoey.

"Not again," Tina groaned.

"Eve doesn't even like Mariah Carey." Deon shook his head. "At least she has a good voice."

"How many times are we gonna have to hear this song?" Tina covered her ears and glanced out at the crowd. A wave of realization washed over her as she watched the teens sway together, entranced. Zoey had a reason for everything she did, and was always a step ahead with her evil bidding. She didn't just invite the entire 10th grade to cause chaos or secure her space as a popular girl. This Christmas party was supposed to be an undercover exorcism, but now, the demon Zozo was going to use the party to get the rest of their graduating class to follow her instead.

"Oh my gosh, Deon," Tina said, grabbing his arm. "She's using the song to lull everyone into submission!"

"I think you're right," Deon said. "Something tells me we're gonna hear this song again if we don't stop them."

"We have to do something," Tina said. "I don't know if I can handle hearing this song on repeat."

Deon winced and covered his ears. "Why won't she stop singing?"

Tina stared out into the sea of complacent faces. Zoey had everyone at the party completely entranced as she repeated the poppy Christmas tune again and again.

"I think she's using the song to hypnotize everyone," Tina said. "Remember what Celeste said about the demon and chanting?"

"I think you're right," Deon said. "So what do we do?"

Tina held her hands to her ears. The demon was

ruining her favorite Christmas song. "We have to play something else. Something that will snap them out of it."

"You take the mic, I can DJ," Deon said. "I think I can get Chris out of the way. He's totally zoned out. "

Tina nodded. "Okay."

"What do you wanna sing?"

What *did* Tina want to sing? Unlike her friends, Tina was not very confident when it came to performing in front of a crowd. But she needed to do something to snap the zombified student body out of their trance. Even though she didn't want the partygoers to trash her house, and she was terrified of being perceived by others, she couldn't let Zoey possess the entire 10th grade en masse.

Tina flipped through the karaoke booklet to the "T" section. The only song she truly knew by heart wasn't a Christmas song, but it was a banger, a bass thumping party song that was sure to get everyone going again. Tina, Eve, and Lacey had spent all summer when she was twelve practicing this song back and forth. Tina's heart squeezed as she remembered jumping up and down on Lacey's bed at one of their sleepovers, rapping the lyrics into a pink handled hairbrush turned microphone. It was the perfect track to breathe some life back into the zombified students, a real party pleaser.

"That one," Tina said, pointing at the list.

Deon scrunched up his face. "Are you sure?"

Tina nodded. "Definitely."

"Okay, then." Deon stepped up to the karaoke booth as Eve finished her set.

Tina took the microphone and pushed Eve out of the way. She had to act fast before Zoey could interfere. Fortunately, when it came to setting up karaoke tracks, Deon was a quick draw sharp shooter.

"Hit it, Deon!" Tina shouted.

Deon pressed a series of buttons on the board and rhythmic bass boomed through the house. The lyrics for Tag Team's *Whoomp! There It Is!* flashed on the screen, though she didn't need the words to sing along. Tina sucked in a deep breath and rapped into the microphone like her life depended on it. She only knew the words to the radio edit version of the song, the one with the bad lyrics bleeped out, but it didn't matter. Tina faked her confidence long enough, and one by one, the hypnotized students seemed to snap out of their haze. Flickers of recognition shone in their eyes as Tina belted out the rap lyrics she knew by heart.

"Yeah!" one of the boys shouted, pumping his fist in the air in a circular motion. "Whooo!"

Two other girls began to dance and jump around. Bottles of Zima clinked together and hands waved in the air like they just didn't care. Someone even raised a lit lighter up in appreciation. It was working; she was bringing everyone back from Zoey's hypnosis. Tina smiled as adrenaline coursed through her veins. She was doing it!

Her gaze flicked to the karaoke screen, a never ending stream of BOOM SHAKA LAKA lyrics scrolled up the screen faster and faster as if someone had pushed the fast forward button on a VCR. And then, before Tina could launch into the fourth stanza, everything came to a screeching halt. The backing music cut out, the karaoke machine went dead, and everyone stopped cheering. Tina stared at her reflection in the karaoke machine screen, and her blood turned to ice. The black, hovering mass was back, resting on her right shoulder in the reflection from the karaoke screen like a terrifying, oversized parrot. Over her left shoulder, the true reflection of the ghoulish demon Zozo grinned at her with a mouth full of razor-sharp teeth.

Tina pivoted to face the terror at her back, her body

moving slowly, weighed down by fear. Zoey was behind the DJ booth now, Deon and Chris sprawled under the Christmas tree in a daze. Her eyes were wide with fury, and the garish demon within flickered to the surface, its features blending in with Lacey's, morphing and shifting like melted wax. Something was happening. The creature seemed to be getting weaker. At this rate, the demon wouldn't be able to hold the facade of Zoey in Lacey Dennison's skin for much longer.

Zoey cleared her throat and shook her head. Lacey's beautiful features returned to the demon's face and for a moment, the demon Zozo's true form was concealed again. She held up a giant red velvet Santa sack and gazed into Tina's eyes, her pupils dilated, dark and piercing.

"Okay, everyone!" Zoey said. "It's *present* time!"

Chapter Twelve

Tina's would-be exorcism was turning into the Christmas party from hell. All of the snacks had been devoured, and garbage littered every free surface of the kitchen counter. Someone kept lighting up menthol cigarettes making the smoke alarm go off. At some point, the music started again and Metallica's *Creeping Death* replaced the rap music. Her dining room table had been overturned, and a mini mosh pit formed where she usually did her homework and ate mac n' cheese.

Tina and Deon huddled together at the edge of the chaos, dodging red plastic cups and the occasional sneaker as debris flew through the air. The smell of sweaty teenage bodies and a various blend of colognes, body sprays, and perfumes mingled together in a gag-inducing musk. Even though it was cold outside, Tina's house was heating up by the minute. The party was building to a fever pitch, and if Tina and Deon didn't intervene soon, something bad was sure to happen.

"What do we do?" Deon shouted to Tina through the noise. His usually confident, assured demeanor was long gone. Like Tina, he looked scared as hell, and couldn't seem to hide it anymore.

"No idea," Tina said. "Man, I wish Celeste was here to help us."

"Too late now," Deon said.

The sound of a screeching microphone cut through the noise. Zoey had the karaoke microphone gripped in her taloned hand. She tapped on the mic, and, like magic, regained the attention of the high schoolers. The music stopped playing. The moshers in the mosh pit stopped moshing. Every single partygoer stopped what they were doing to listen. The demon was in full control.

"Marquise Johnson, Santa brought something special for you!" Zoey held a hand up to shield her eyes and gazed out into the rowdy crowd. "*I seeeeee you!*"

Every single face in the crowd was turned up toward Zoey, glassy eyed and smiling, hanging on the demon's every word. Tina and Deon hugged the living room wall, trying in vain to disappear. Tina realized woefully too late that she had not planned her Christmas party well. To be fair, she didn't anticipate having a house full of uninvited classmates, and she certainly didn't anticipate Zoey spearheading a demonic gift exchange.

"Come on, Marquise!" Zoey said, her voice singsongy and high-pitched. "Your present is waiting! Don't be shy!"

"I'll come up!" Chastity Baker shouted. "Is there a present in there for me?"

"*I've got a present for you.*" A voice snickered.

Laughter pealed through the crowd.

Chastity threw a disgusted, red-faced glare in the direction of the voice. "Shut up, Caleb!"

"Calm down," Zoey said. "Everyone, wait your turn. There's something in here for all of you."

Tina peered over the heads of dozens of eager teen faces to read the time on her kitchen clock. It was already after ten. She had less than two hours left to cue up the camcorder, recite the incantation, and trap the demon Zozo. They were cutting it too close for time, and if Lance didn't hurry up with the camcorder, their whole exorcism party would be a bust. Why didn't she just dip into her used car fund and buy a camcorder for herself in the first place?

Marquise stepped up to the microphone, still queasy-looking from his Zima induced barf-o-rama. Before that night, Tina hadn't said a word to the broad-shouldered teen. Marquise ran with a different crowd than she did, but other than barfing on her floor, it seemed like he was an otherwise good guy. Whatever Zoey had in store for him, it wasn't going to be good.

"What do I do?" Marquise asked.

"Reach your hand inside the bag," Zoey instructed, her voice high-pitched and baby cute. "And grab a present."

"How do I know which present is for me?" Marquise asked.

"The bag will know the right gift to give you," Zoey said. "Go ahead. Just pick one."

Marquise shrugged, reached his hand inside the bag, and pulled out a small square box wrapped in red- and green-striped paper.

"Go ahead," Zoey said, her voice rushed and impatient. "*Open it.*"

Marquise gave a skeptical half-smile-half-frown and tore into the gift. The red- and green-striped paper fell away to reveal a brand new Magic 8 Ball toy inside.

"A bowling ball?" Marquise scratched his chin. "What am I supposed to do with this?"

"It's not a bowling ball!" Zoey growled, took in a deep breath, and closed her eyes. "It's a Magic 8 Ball, of course. Ask it a question, and it will tell you the future."

"Psh, yeah right." Marquise handed it back. "No thanks, I don't need this kid's stuff."

"Oh, but I think you do." Zoey's eyes glowed. She pushed the Magic 8 Ball back into his hands and her voice dipped again, low and gruff and monstrous. "*Ask a question.*"

"Whatever." Marquise rolled his eyes and scoffed again. "Is this party gonna get any better?"

He shook the Magic 8 Ball and gazed into the viewing area. Inky water sloshed around inside the black plastic toy billiards ball. From her angle, Tina could just barely make out the triangular shaped indicator in the viewing window as it bubbled to the surface. Marquis opened his mouth and read the words.

"IT IS DECIDEDLY SO."

Marquise grunted and the Magic 8 Ball fell from his hands. Tina gasped as his eyes flashed and his discontented expression melted away. His usually cool guy demeanor was replaced with the vacant stare that Chris and Eve and all of the other demonites displayed. It was then that Tina truly realized what was going on at her impromptu Christmas party that night. Zoey's gift wasn't just some silly kids toy. Her gift was possession.

"Who's next!" Zoey pushed Marquise back into the crowd. He stumbled, zombie-like, back toward his Zima-blasted buddies. "Caleb!"

Tina glanced out into the crowd and anguish pierced her heart. Every single teen was enraptured, eyes glued to the scene and totally unaware of their impending fate. Zoey had everyone hypnotized all over again. If Lance didn't get there soon, she would have a house full of nothing but demonic teens and Zima barf.

Caleb Purdue strutted up to the microphone, gangly and smirking and full of bravado. Despite having a big mouth, the heckler from the crowd was probably the shortest kid in 10th grade. Caleb didn't waste any time and confidently dug his present out of the Santa sack. He ripped the red- and green-striped paper away and revealed a square, multicolored box.

"Oh hell yeah! Rubik's Cube!" Caleb began to twist the square segments. "Yo, dawg, I used to be so good at this!"

Caleb twisted the Rubik's Cube three times. Just like Marquise, his eyes flashed, his swagger diminished, and he turned into another member of the demonic horde.

"This is getting out of hand," Deon whispered. "The next time Zoey is distracted, we need to make a run for it."

"Okay. Deal."

"Oh, I've got two matching presents this time!" Zoey said, pulling two rectangular boxes from the bag. "Joseph, Joshua, come get your gifts!"

The Bruner twins, Joseph and Joshua, hustled to the karaoke mic. Zoey handed the boys the boxes, which they each opened without enthusiasm. Something told Tina they were used to getting matching gifts. However, when they ripped away the red- and green-striped paper, their expressions lit up in mirror image expressions of joy.

"A GAME BOY!"

The crowd whooped as they opened the boxes and powered up the handheld video games. So far, this was the best present yet. Where was Zoey getting all the money for these gifts? And how many more were in the bag?

"Man, I haven't played this in, like, forever!" Joshua said.

"What if we—" Joseph froze.

Just like the other boys before them, the Bruner twins' expressions fell flat, their vacant eyes glowed, and all signs of their former personalities were wiped away.

"That's it. Time for Plan B," Deon said.

"Wait, we don't have one!" Tina whisper-shouted. "What's Plan B?!"

"Run like hell."

Deon grabbed Tina's hand and pulled her away from the wall. Her legs were jelly and her brain felt like it might explode. What had she gotten them into? Why hadn't she planned this thing better? And where the heck was Lance at?

"Okay, who's next?" Zoey trilled into the microphone. The demon turned to face Tina and Deon as they skirted past the Christmas tree. "Ah, there you are."

Deon froze, still as a statue.

"D! Run!" Tina shouted. "Keep going!"

"*Deon.*" Zoey threw them a razor sharp smile, her voice dripping with poisoned honey. "You're up next."

Chapter Thirteen

A string of multicolored Christmas lights flew through the air, encircling Tina's chest like a lasso. She was yanked backward and spun around and around, the string lights pulling tighter and tighter against her chest. A blur of demonic faces and Christmas decorations spun before her eyes and a wave of nausea hit hard. The spinning stopped as bile gurgled up in her throat.

"Not so fast, Tiny!" Zoey squealed. "You'll want to see this."

Zoey's boyfriend, Chris, held the end of the Christmas string lights. He stood next to her like a zombie, with Tina as his dog on an illuminated leash. Tina was properly trapped now, with zero chance of escape. She cursed herself for not running when she had the chance.

Eve emerged from the crowd, smiling and bubbly. Even in her tied up state, Tina still couldn't get over her friend's demonic transformation. Under the silver eyeshadow and bubblegum pink lip gloss, Eve's unnatural beauty was fading. Just like with Zoey, every now and then, the sallow skinned, sharp-toothed demon facade slipped through, revealing the true horror just beneath her skin.

Deon, powerless under Zoey's influence, had no choice but to go along with their plan. Eve took him by the hand and led him to the big red Santa bag where a fiendish-looking Zoey was waiting. He turned and gave Tina one last hopeless glance.

"I'm counting on you, T," he said. "See you on the other side."

Tina struggled in her binds, glancing in vain at the front door. Where the hell was Lance anyway? She had to think of something else. With Deon as a soon-to-be part of the horde, she only had herself to rely on.

Zoey pulled a red- and green-striped gift from the bag. "To: Deon. Love: Santa. Oh, this is an extra special gift for you!"

Deon took the gift and glanced up at Eve. A single tear trailed down his cheek as he unwrapped the gift. The Christmas wrapping paper fell away to reveal a circular wheel with large red, blue, yellow, and green buttons. The dreaded, anxiety-induced electronic Simon game.

"Tell you what, Deon." Zoey cackled. "You play the game and win, and we'll let you go."

"It's a trap," Deon said. "No one can win this game."

Zoey pouted and her mouth elongated. Her eyes glowed red and her cheekbones jutted out like two sharp knobs on the side of her face. "But I love to play games."

"Enough!" Tina said. "Let them go! It's me you want."

"Wrong." Tina giggled. "I want them *all*. We *need* them all. The souls of teenage boys are so delicious, and my demons and I are starving."

A new feeling of dread sunk in her chest. She glanced around the room and realized that the only people to have gotten gifts from Zoey that night were of the masculine persuasion. Tina had gotten it all wrong. Zoey didn't want to turn everyone at school into demons;

just the girls. The boys were going to meet an even worse fate than possession. Demons needed to feed, and boys were on the menu.

"You're going to eat them?" Tina shouted.

"No. Just their souls." Zoey shrugged. "So, what'll it be, D? Gonna play the game?"

Deon gave Eve one last yearning glance. He powered on the electronic Simon toy. It beeped and flashed to life in his hand, the formerly cheerful 8-bit music now a death knell. One by one, the lights illuminated and beeped, and Deon had to focus to remember and repeat the sequence. With every round, the beeping lights became more complicated to remember, the pattern moving faster. Sweat dripped from Deon's forehead onto the electronic device as it lit up and beeped in his hand. And then...

BUUUURRRRR

Deon failed to repeat the correct repetition of flashes and beeps. The Simon toy fell to the ground with an awful, plastic crash. His eyes flashed and the anguish melted from his face into a blank expression of pure nothing. Tina was truly alone now in the fight against Zoey and her horde of demons.

"Gavin Lundquist, you're up next!" Zoey squealed.

The crowd cheered. Chris raised his hands up to join them, robotic and mirroring their emotions. He had dropped the end of the Christmas light cord in his mock enthusiasm. Zoey was distracted as he ushered Gavin, the 10th grade class president, onto the stage. This was Tina's chance to escape.

Tina edged slowly into the crowd of bodies and joined in with the cheers. In her peripherals she caught Eve and Deon, together again at last, sporting twin dead expressions and glowing eyes. It wasn't supposed to be this way. Lance had clearly stood her up, and now her only other non-possessed friend was, well, possessed. Tina needed to get to her bedroom and figure out a way to salvage this night and complete the exorcism. As long as Zoey was still standing over the pentagram before midnight, and as long as Tina recited the incantation, the exorcism would work. She just had to think of something else to trap the demon in.

And that's when Tina remembered.

Zoey and Lacey staring at their demonic reflections.

The importance of appearance, the obsession with fashion and style and perfection.

Vanity.

Celeste said she needed to appeal to their weakness.

But what could Tina possibly use to trap Zoey in? As she pushed her way through the crowd toward her bedroom, her and Lacey's favorite movie came to mind. In *Return to Oz*, Dorothy had to help Ozma escape from the mirror. Ozma had been trapped in the mirror by an evil enchantress, and only Dorothy could help her get out. If mirrors could trap Alice while she was in Wonderland, and if they could trap Ozma in Oz, could a mirror trap the demon Zozo too?

Chapter Fourteen

"**H**ey, the bedrooms are off limits!"

Tina unwound the Christmas lights from her chest as a boy and girl she didn't know jumped from the edge of her bed. She ushered them out of her room and closed the door, trying not to be grossed out by the fact that they were making out on her bed. She shuddered to think of what might be going on in her mother's bedroom.

"Mirror, mirror, where do I have mirrors?" Tina muttered to herself.

Even though Tina was not particularly invested in her appearance, she still managed to have mirrors everywhere. Her vanity mirror and the bathroom mirror were too big. Then, her gaze landed on the antique silver-handled mirror on her dresser; the special, vintage Victorian-style mirror with matching fancy hair brush that had belonged to her great-grandmother.

"Sorry, Great Grandma Maddie," Tina said, lifting up the hefty handheld mirror. "But I need to use this."

Tina went to her desk and grabbed a roll of Santa print wrapping paper, tape, and scissors. She hastily wrapped the odd-shaped present, unsure whether her plan would work or not. If she could get Zoey to stare at her own hideous reflection long enough, Tina could recite the incantation and hopefully trap the demon in the mirror. She didn't have a better idea. Deon was possessed and Lance hadn't shown up. This was her last shot at reversing all of the damage that came out of her Sweet Sixteen party. Every single possessed student in that room was in danger and it was all because she wanted to have a little fun with her friends at her birthday party. Their fates and very lives depended on her not screwing this thing up.

She placed her hand on the doorknob and nearly turned it when a thought crossed her mind. What if it *didn't* work? What would become of her then? Would her consciousness be trapped somewhere again, like when she and Eve were stuck in the dARiA*'s catalog? Or would she be trapped in her own mind and forced to experience all of the awful things that Zoey and her horde got up to? Being a prisoner inside her own body, stripped of agency, was probably the worst possible thing she could imagine.

One little magic mirror Christmas present wasn't going to be enough. What if Eve swooped in and tried to stop her too? Tina glanced at her backpack purse and remembered that she had one last mirror. She dug out her CoverGirl pressed powder compact, shoved it in her back pocket, and rejoined the Christmas party.

Zoey was still busy with her gift exchange when Tina weaved through the crowd. Miguel Montana was at the karaoke mic holding a Bop It electronic game in his hand. Just like before, Zoey instructed him to play the game, and as soon as Miguel failed, all semblance of humanity left his eyes and was replaced with an otherworldly light.

"Tina!" A familiar voice called her name from behind. She turned and for a brief moment, hope entered her heart. Lance stood in the doorway, bug-eyed as he took in the rowdy party scene.

"Lance!" Tina spun around, leaned in and hugged

him. After the night she had, it was good to see a friend. "I almost thought you wouldn't make it!"

"My mom's car wouldn't start," he said. "I had to skate here. Sorry I'm late. I brought the camcorder though."

"We're running out of time," Tina said. "Look. The demons are getting weaker."

Lance followed her line of vision toward the karaoke mic. Zoey and Eve were indeed looking rough. The nubs on the side of their faces were more pronounced than ever, and their razor sharp, yellow teeth protruded from elongated jaws.

"Yikes," he said. "Okay, I'm hyped. Let's do this thing!"

"I've got the blank VHS tapes and a can of salt stashed on top of the TV," Tina said. "I'm going to give this present to Zoey to distract her."

"What's up with the presents?" Lance asked.

Tina groaned. "You don't wanna know."

"I see we have a special guest!" Zoey's shrill voice pierced through the air. Tina's hackles stood on end. They'd been spotted.

"Oh crap, change of plan," Tina said. "Whatever you do, do NOT accept a present from them."

"Oh, Lance!" Zoey taunted. "Lancey-boy! We've got something special for you up here!"

"Wait!" Tina said, holding her gift high. "I want you to open your present first!"

Zoey's wicked features softened. "A present? For me?"

Tina flicked her gaze to the TV and whispered to Lance. "Start recording!"

"Got it." Lance gave her a thumbs up.

Tina clutched the present, her heart beating fast. Zoey might have been vain and greedy, but she wasn't dumb. The demon always seemed to be a step ahead of Tina. If Lacey really was still in there, somewhere deep down, perhaps now would be the time to reach her, when the veil was nearly at its thinnest. Maybe she could appeal to her trapped friend, and not the demon, just long enough to set her plan in motion.

"Lacey, do you remember when we were little girls and we would sing into our hairbrushes?" Tina asked.

The demon blinked. For a moment, Tina swore that she saw a flicker of her friend staring back at her through the demon's eyes. "Of course I do!"

"Well, since we have the karaoke machine set up," Tina said, "I thought, well, maybe we could sing our favorite song together one last time."

Tina handed the wrapped mirror to Zoey, hoping she would take the bait. It wasn't exactly the same shape and size as the matching hair brush, but it was close enough. Hopefully whatever was left of Lacey in there would be endeared by the memory of their hairbrush karaoke microphone days. A low snarl escaped from the demon's thin, graying lips as it took the present from Tina.

"It's too late for a Salt N' Peppa duet now, Tiny," the demon said. "But I'll open your silly little present anyway."

Tina took a deep breath and crossed her fingers behind her back. Zoey's elongated, taloned fingers shredded the paper with glee, turning the Santa wrapping paper into confetti. She wrapped her claws around the antique silver-handled mirror.

"Oh, Tiny," the demon purred. "I *love* it."

The room seemed to wobble as Tina backed away from the stage. Sparkling dust motes filled the air, and the atmosphere was lighter. *She* felt lighter, almost as though she could launch off the ground and float away. Tina glanced at the kitchen clock; only ten minutes to midnight! If she didn't recite the incantation right then and there, it would be too late.

"A mirror!" Eve shrieked. "I wanna see!"

Eve pushed Tina out of the way and joined Zoey by the microphone. Eve tried to snatch the mirror from Zoey's hand, but the demon growled. Their true visages were even more pronounced now, the demons unable to mask their hideous faces any longer. Zoey and Eve looked more like gargoyles than teen girls as they fought for the mirror.

"I want a turn!" Eve screeched. "Let me have it!"

"It's mine!" Zoey snarled.

No one moved as the two demons battled it out over the mirror. The Christmas party had come to a halt, every single hypnotized face staring up at the scene. Tina saw regular teens and demons through the sea of faces, each unblinking and unmoving as if under a spell. Dozens and dozens of glowing eyes staring up at their master, awaiting her command.

"Lance, are you getting this?"

Tina was relieved to see Lance peering through the viewfinder with one eye, his other eye squinted closed. He gave her a thumbs-up of approval. The camera was rolling. The demons were distracted. All she needed now was ...

Oh crap.

Where did she put the salt?

Tina shoved her way through the sea of mannequin-still bodies toward the TV stand where she had a canister of salt stashed. All she needed to do was make a circle around them, and then she would be able to start reading the incantation. Tina opened the cabinet door where her VHS tapes were stored and grabbed the salt, when the most horrible, shrill sound filled the air.

AIYEEEEEE!!!!

The hair on Tina's neck stood at attention as she glanced at the makeshift karaoke stage. Zoey had gotten control of the mirror, and was gazing lovingly into the glass. Eve tugged at Zoey's arm with a pair of monstrous claws, with fiery, glowing eyes and spittle flying from her lips.

"Give it to me!" Eve shrieked.

Eve gave one last tug, and Tina's antique mirror ejected from Zoey's hand. The mirror launched through the air and time slowed as it suspended in the sparkling Winter Solstice night. The mirror flipped around and around, turning over and over again, reflecting the horrific faces of the guests at Tina's Christmas party. Tina caught her own reflection in the mirror for a brief moment as it sailed overhead, her lips open wide in an "O" of surprise. The mirror tumbled over and over again, sailing through the living room until it connected with the wall and shattered.

Chapter Fifteen

Tina was petrified, frozen still as the other mannequin demon teens. She didn't dare to move a muscle as Zoey and Eve set their evil sights on her. In any other circumstance, she would have been upset that her great-grandmother's mirror had broken—and she was—but not for sentimental reasons. Without the demons being distracted, Tina had no clue how she would keep them at bay as she drew the salted circle of protection.

"Oh look, Tiny is getting salty with us again," Zoey mocked. "Whatcha gonna do with that? Season us?"

Tina frowned, her hand squeezing the salt canister as the fear left her body. What was the point of having her house trashed, letting Deon get turned into a walking demon snack, and basically ending her very existence if she was too afraid to fight back? Tina might have been meek and mild in the past, but not anymore. She wasn't going to let herself be bullied, even by demons masquerading as her two best friends.

"Come on, T," Eve said. "Make this easy. We need our best friend to join us!"

"Good things come in threes," Zoey purred. "When you join us, we'll be unstoppable!"

"We'll rule the school, T!" Eve said. "And we can feast on the delicious souls of every boy in sight."

The thought of herself dressed in the latest dARiA*s fashions, demonic like one of them as they slow-walked down the hall at Tropic Acres High, flashed before her eyes. They were going to walk the halls together as friends again, but demon-free, and on her terms. Tina poured a mound of salt into the palm of her hand and smiled.

"You forgot one thing," she said. "I don't really like boys."

With a flick of her wrist, Tina flung the grains of salt directly in the demon's eyes. Zoey and Eve roared in pain, covering their horrific faces with bony claws. The flesh on their cheekbones and neck melted away behind their talons, leaving burned, meaty patches with open sores that looked a little too much like Freddy Krueger skin.

"My face!" Eve trilled.

Tina didn't waste another moment. She pulled the pressed powder compact from her back pocket and flipped it open, pointing the mirrored side at the demons like a shield. The demons shrieked and writhed as she encircled the karaoke stand with a thick barrier of salt. They hovered inches from Tina's face, hissing and snarling, but too enamored with their own reflections to stop Tina in her tracks.

"You were never good enough for us anyway," Zoey screeched.

"Shut up!" Tina said, pouring out salt like her life depended on it.

"Lacey didn't love you," Eve taunted. "She barely even liked you as a friend!"

"Eve only tolerated you," Zoey cackled. "There was no chance in *hell* you could ever be popular like us."

Tina kept her focus on the salt circle as Zoey and Eve regained their senses. It was almost midnight and she couldn't waste any time bickering with the demons.

Just as she had hoped, the compact mirror did the trick to entice and distract the demons just enough to let her complete the protection circle.

"Popularity is overrated," Tina said. "Time to end this party."

Tina stood tall and pulled up the sleeve of her sweater. The lettering had a slight glow to it earlier in the night. Now, the smudged pen letters shone like a Lite Brite toy, the words glowing as if they were lit within by fire. She had been memorizing those words since Celeste gave them to her, studying and cramming like this was the finals for Demonology 101. She couldn't fail this time. This time, the exorcism and spell reversal had to work. With the compact mirror still pointed at them like a magical amulet or cross, Tina recited the words.

Daemon revertetur ad regnum tuum
Daemon revertetur ad regnum tuum
Daemon revertetur ad regnum tuum

"Oh, really?" Zoey snorted, and propped her hands on her hips. "*Demon return to your realm,* do you know how typical and pathetic you sound?"

Daemonium tibi obligo
Daemonium tibi obligo

Daemonium tibi obligo

"Do you even *know* how to read Latin?" Zoey snorted. "You can't bind me. This is ridiculous."

Demonium mitto te in hoc objectum

Demonium mitto te in hoc objectum

Demonium mitto te in hoc objectum

"Object? What object?" Zoey cackled. "You don't have a Ouija board, dummy! You can't cast me into shit!"

"No, but I can cast you into a VHS tape," Tina said, pointing to the camcorder.

Zoey and Eve followed the direction of Tina's pointed finger.

Lance waved from behind the eyepiece.

"Smile," Tina said. "You're on candid camera!"

"Me! On TV!" Eve said. "Oh, I've always wanted to be on TV!"

"No, you idiot!" Zoey shouted. "Don't look at the …"

But it was too late. The notion of being filmed was too irresistible to the vain demons. Just like with the mirror, Zoey and Eve were moths to the camera flame. They pulled their prettiest demon smiles, fluffed their stringy hair, and flexed their claws.

The clock struck midnight, and Zoey and Eve let out one last lingering howl of pain. Their bodies shuddered and convulsed as their feet lifted off the ground. Tina held back tears as the bodies of her two best friends writhed in pain, the demons within refusing to let go of their cozy human shells.

"Tina!" Lance called out. "Is it working?"

"I don't know!" Tina shouted.

"It's pulling the camera into the circle!" Lance shouted. "I don't know how much longer I can hold on!"

What went wrong? Tina had recited the incantation just as Celeste instructed, and right before midnight. Maybe she was too late? Maybe she missed her window of opportunity. Then, Tina remembered something else that Celeste had said.

What matters is intention, and performing the ritual with love. You must be brave and have heart if you want to release your friends.

Bravery and heart. Tina wasn't athletic like Lacey, or cool like Eve, but heart was one thing she definitely had. Bravery was something she'd had to learn over the past six months. When it came to helping her friends, Tina knew she couldn't wimp out. She had to be brave.

"Lacey! Eve! Fight it!" Tina said. "Take your bodies back! They belong to you!"

Zoey and Eve thrashed in the air, the demonic entities stretching away from their bodies like string cheese or bubblegum, then snapping back and latching on again. The camcorder was working like a vacuum for demon souls, and every time it seemed like Zozo and the demon inside of Eve were about to be sucked in, they held on even more tightly to their earthly bodies. Tina had to do something to help the process along.

Even though the demons couldn't cross the salt barrier that Tina had laid out, she could. Only, as soon as she was inside the circle, Tina would no longer be protected. She didn't know how much longer the incantation would last or how long Lance could hold out hanging on to the camcorder like it was some kind of Ghostbusters trap. She had to take her chances.

Tina lunged over the circle and approached the floating demonic bodies. With her right arm around Eve, and her left arm around Zoey, Tina gathered her best friends into a writhing group hug. The force created by the incantation continued to pull them toward the camcorder, but nothing seemed to break the connection that Zozo had on her friends. The demons snarled and spit, gnashing their teeth and scratching at her, but Tina refused to give up her friends.

"Lacey! Eve! I love you!" she cried out. "Come back to me!"

A flash of light burst from inside the circle of their embrace. The bodies of her friends went limp in her arms. Too heavy for Tina to hold up, her unconscious friends fell to the ground. The camcorder made a *zip, snap* sound, and the VHS tape ejected from the smoking camcorder with a hiss. The atmosphere wobbled, the air flexing in and out as if the room took a deep breath.

And then, the party was all over.

And it was done.

Chapter Sixteen

"Party's over folks! Time to go home."

Tina opened her front door and motioned for her uninvited guests to exit. She ushered out dozens of confused teens into the chilly Winter Solstice night air. The glow of her exterior Christmas decorations illuminated the faces of the stumbling party goers, many still dizzy from months of Zoey's possession and mind control. Every single teen at the party was left scratching their heads, wondering what the heck had just happened. Everyone except for Tina and Lance, that is. No one seemed to remember anything that happened at the party at all.

"Thanks for coming. Make sure you have a designated driver," Tina said. "Merry Christmas."

Lacey and Eve sat under the Christmas tree, stunned and sobbing as Tina pushed the last party guest out the door. Deon wandered over to Eve, still in a haze from his own possession. Lance stood rigid against the wall with an expression somewhere between confusion, wonder and relief. Tina's house was absolutely trashed, but the worst was over. The demon Zozo was trapped safe and sound in a VHS tape and her best friends were back.

Tina glanced out her living room window up into the Winter Solstice sky. A single star shone brightly in the dark, as though it were winking down at her. Tina winked back. "Thanks for everything, Celeste."

"Who were you talking to?" Lance handed her the VHS tape. "Careful, this thing is hot."

"No one." Tina took the tape. The plastic casing was warm in her hands. "Thanks."

"What happened?" Lacey asked. "And why is your house decorated for Christmas?"

"You've been gone for a while," Tina said.

"Ew, and why am I wearing pink velour?" Eve tugged at her bubblegum colored zip-up hoodie. "Yuck."

Tina bent down to Lacey's level. "Remember playing Light as a Feather, Stiff as a Board?"

"Yeah."

"Well, that was months ago," Tina said. "You've been possessed since my birthday party. It's December 21st."

Lacey glanced down at her clothes. "Am I wearing a crop top?"

"Yeah." Tina laughed. "The demon who possessed you had some interesting fashion choices."

"Wait, so was I possessed too?" Eve asked.

Deon took Eve's hand and helped her up. "Yeah, but only for a few days."

"You all keep saying the word 'possessed,'" Lacey said. "What do you mean?"

"Like, glowing eyes, took over your body, tried to take over the whole school. Demonic mean-girl level 'possessed.' That's what we mean," Deon said. "It was pretty bad."

"I think I do remember something," Lacey said. "But I thought it was a dream. I remember feeling trapped. Like I wanted to move and speak, but I couldn't."

"Me too," Eve said. "Oh my gosh, Tina. Your house. It looks awful."

Tina shrugged. "I had a Christmas party. It's to be expected."

"Wait, so, did you help us get back?" Lacey asked.

"Yeah. Deon and Lance helped too," Tina said. "The demon is trapped in a VHS tape now. I had to recite an incantation before the Winter Solstice began. It's no big deal."

"No big deal?" Eve said. "Tina, can you hear yourself? We could have all been lost forever if it wasn't for you."

"I guess," Tina said. "I just wanted my friends back."

"I remember hearing your voice while I was stuck inside myself," Lacey said. "All I wanted was to be with my friends and family again. You did it, Tina. You saved us."

Tina, Lacey, and Eve embraced in a group hug, and for the first time in months, Tina allowed herself to let go. She didn't have to be on guard anymore, didn't have to worry and wonder if everything would turn out okay. She cried into her friends' hair and held them tight. The Christmas wish she made at the mall came true. If board game demons could be real, then maybe Santa was real, too.

After a good long while, the friends finally let go and wiped their tears away.

"So, what now?" Lacey asked. "How do I go back to my normal life after all of this?"

"I don't think anyone remembers anything," Tina said. "You have some lost time to make up for, but otherwise, you should be good."

"The demon was a pretty good student," Eve said. "I think your grades are still okay."

"It even made sure you kept up on softball practice," Tina snorted. "Zoey was a real bitch though."

"She called herself Zoey?" Lacey asked. "Weird."

"For now, let's get you home and rested," Tina said. "We can sort out everything else after the holidays."

"Thanks, Tina." Lacey leaned in for another long, tight hug. "I love you so much. You'll always be my best friend."

Tina's heart clenched. "I love you too, Lace."

"Come on, I've got my dad's van. I can drive you ladies home," Deon said. "I'm way past curfew, though, so we gotta jet. Lance, can you help me grab this karaoke stuff?"

"Sure thing, dude," he said. "Can you give me a ride home too?"

"Definitely."

"Call me tomorrow, okay?" Lacey blew Tina a kiss and waved. "Thanks again for everything. I owe you my life."

"Thanks, T," Eve said, snagging one last hug. "I'm sorry I got turned into a demonite and you had to do this all alone."

"I wasn't all alone," Tina said, glancing at Deon and Lance. "I had a little help from my friends."

"A little?" Deon scoffed. "I almost turned into a demonic Capri Sun. What do you mean a little?"

"Capri Sun?" Eve asked, her eyebrow arched.

"Don't ask. They were going to slurp the souls of all the boys in the tenth grade or something," Tina said.

"Don't you want some help cleaning up?" Lance asked.

"No, I got it. You guys go home before you get in trouble," Tina said. "Involving our parents in this mess is the last thing we need."

"True that," Deon said. "Okay, let's get this gear and go."

Tina grabbed the karaoke mic and helped her friends load up the van. After Lacey, Eve and Deon were loaded in the van, Lance headed back into the house.

"Almost forgot my camcorder," he said.

"Ooh, right." Tina cringed. "Is it broken?"

Lance shrugged. "Probably. It's no sweat. I'll just ask Santa to bring me a new one for Christmas."

"Har har."

Lance smirked and scratched the bridge of his nose. "So about what you said back there, before you melted those demons' faces? That thing about not liking boys?"

"Oh, right," Tina said. "What about it?"

"Do you not like them in general?" He winced. "Or romantically?"

"I guess I don't know." Tina shrugged. "I thought I liked girls, but I met someone recently and, I dunno. Maybe I just like the person and it doesn't matter if they are a boy or a girl?"

"Cool, cool." Lance glanced down at his feet.

"Anyway, I'm still trying to figure that part out," Tina said. "But I don't hate all boys if that's what you mean. I like Deon as a friend, for sure. And ... I like you, too."

"Maybe after Christmas we can go skate together or something," he said. "Hang out, you know. As friends."

Tina smiled. "Sounds rad."

"Cool." Lance sighed. "Well, they're waiting for me. Thanks for including me in all this. I never thought I would see an exorcism for real."

"Thanks for being my cameraman," Tina said.

"Couldn't have done all this without you."

"You're pretty cool—"

"For a girl?" Tina smirked.

"No. Just pretty cool."

"You're pretty cool too."

Tina leaned in and gave Lance a long hug. This hug felt different, and she knew why. Maybe after the dust settled with Lacey, the possession, and the holidays, Tina could explore that feeling. For now, she was just grateful to have her friends and her peace of mind.

"Merry Christmas, Tina," Lance said, pulling away. "Catch you on the flip."

Tina laughed. "Catch you on the flip."

She shut the door behind him and bolted the lock. The last bit of adrenaline she had been running on for hours drained from her body, and it took everything she had just to fall into bed. Christmas party cleanup would have to wait. With her clothes and shoes still on, Tina drifted off to sleep, secure in the knowledge that everything was set right, and that even though she was growing up, there was still a little bit of magic to be found in the world.

Epilogue

"How's Colorado?"

Tina held her new black cordless phone to her ear as she pushed start on the dishwasher. It took hours, but after cleaning her house all morning, all signs of the demonic Christmas party had been swept and wiped clean. All except for the pentagram that was now engraved in her living room floor. Something had happened during the exorcism to permanently etch the emblem into her floor. Tina hoped her mother never removed the area rug. She would have some explaining to do.

"Oh, it's wonderful!" Her mother cooed in her ear. "It's so cold! The snow is just beautiful, though. Rick is teaching me how to ski. I'm not half bad."

"That's great, Mom," Tina said.

"You know, I called the Johnsons next door. They said there were quite a few cars at the house last night," her mother said. "You weren't having a party, were you?"

Tina winced. "Not really. Just Lacey and Eve. I was kind of lonely."

"That's fine. I do feel guilty for leaving you around the holidays," her mother said. "But Tina, I have some big news!"

Oh, here we go.

Tina rolled her eyes. "Oh, yeah?"

"Rick asked me to marry him!" she shouted. "We're engaged!"

"That's great, mom," Tina said, trying to muster some positivity. "Congratulations."

"We're going to get married this summer, and oh, you'll be my Maid of Honor in the wedding and—" Her mother was quiet for a moment. "Tina, are you okay with this?"

Tina walked into her bedroom and opened her top dresser draw. There, safely stashed away with her socks and sports bras was the now cursed VHS tape. She probably needed to put the cursed VHS in a safety deposit box, or throw it in a lake or something, but for now, this would have to do. Even looking at the tape creeped her out. She shut the dresser drawer and flopped on her bed.

"Why wouldn't I be?" Tina asked.

"Well, because I know that the divorce has been hard for you—"

"Mom, you deserve to be happy too," Tina said. "Don't worry about me. Please, tell Rick I said congratulations too."

"I love you, Tina," her mom said. "Is your dad on his way to pick you up yet?"

"Yeah, he should be here in a few minutes, actually," she said. "I should go so I can finish packing up my stuff."

"Okay, well, I will call you at his place later," she said. "And I'll see you after Christmas! Oh, I can't wait to show you my engagement ring. It's a huge diamond!"

"That's great, mom," Tina said. "Okay, I gotta go. Talk to you soon."

"Bye!"

Tina pressed the END button on her portable phone and returned it to the cradle in her room. She sighed and picked her packed duffle bag off of her bed, contemplating whether or not to tell her dad about the engagement. It would be hard to keep the secret, but it wasn't hers to tell. Either way, she was looking forward to spending time away with her dad after all the events of the past few days. Just a few days to clear her head and try to get back to normal.

BEEP, BEEP!

Tina walked to the living room window and peered outside. Her dad waved from behind the wheel of his truck. Tina waved back and bumped the Christmas tree with her elbow.

PLINK.

Something metallic hit the ground. Her silver baby ornament had fallen from its placement on the tree. Tina bent down, picked it up and placed it back on the branch.

"There you go," she said, catching her reflection in the mirrored finish.

Tina gasped as she stared into the Christmas ornament. Something hovered over her right shoulder. Something dark and ominous, with sharp teeth and eyes that glowed like fire.

BEEP BEEP!

She jumped and the ornament fell from her hand. This time, it smashed, shattering into a dozen pieces. Tina didn't take the time to clean it up. Her purple boombox on the kitchen counter churned to life, blasting out a slow, demonic sounding version of *Silent Night*. Tina grabbed her duffle bag and slammed the front door behind her as the shattered ornament pieces giggled beneath the Christmas tree.

Acknowledgements

I'd like to start by giving a big THANK YOU to every single reader, reviewer, blogger, and podcaster who enthusiastically shared their love for *Birthday Party Demon*. This sequel wouldn't have been possible without your support. Readers make indie horror great!

Thank you as always to my family for continually supporting my dream. I wouldn't be able to share my stories if I didn't have a great team at my back.

Thank you to my advanced readers, Damien Casey and Heather Paul. I can always count on you two for feedback and I appreciate your friendship and time!

Thank you to my publisher, editor and cover artist Joey Powell for always letting me roll with my weird ideas and turning them into a beautiful book.

And thank YOU reader for being here and spending time with my words!

Don't miss the conclusion of Wendy Dalrymple's Party Demon trilogy!

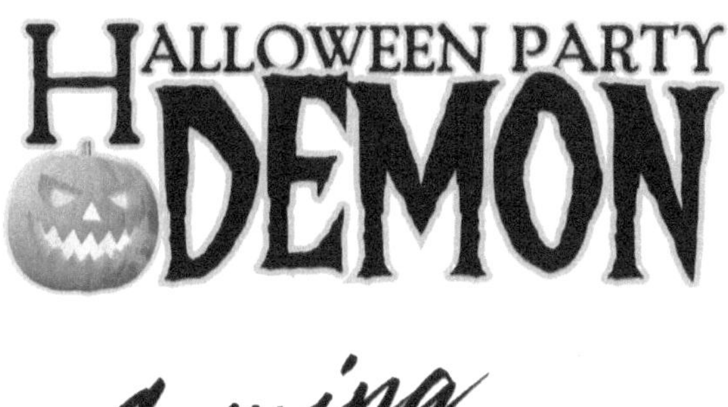

Coming 2021